The Incident

Hanna Akpan

Maybe there's something you're afraid to say or someone you're afraid to love, or somewhere you're afraid to go. It's gonna hurt. It's gonna hurt because it matters.
-- John Green

CONTENTS

The Incident

ONE

It's a rainy, Monday morning, which is typical in Washington. I woke up to the rain hitting my window. I then looked at my phone and saw that it displayed eight forty-five AM. School didn't start until nine forty-five. I got out of bed and went to my bathroom. Then turned on the shower head, so the water would warm up. Looking into the mirror, I rubbed my eyes. My name is Aly Pisano. I'm seventeen years old. There really isn't anything interesting about me. I'm your normal nerdy teenager, who enjoys getting good grades instead of partying with my peers.

I touched my cheek and splashed water on my face. Once finished, I got into the shower. While standing in the shower, my mind started to overthink. After ten minutes passed, I got out of the shower and got dressed. While looking in the mirror, a smile appeared on my face. My outfit was dark-washed American Eagle jeans, a black t-shirt, and white Converse sneakers. I topped it all off with a white, oversized flannel. I grabbed my stuff and headed downstairs to the kitchen. I could smell the turkey bacon and blueberry waffles my mom always made me on the first day of school. I walked in and said, "Good morning, Mom."

She kissed me on the cheek and smiled. "Good morning, Aly," she said, as she flipped the bacon over. "Are you ready for your first day of senior year?" I smiled at her.

In all honesty, I didn't want to go back to school. For the past two years, it has been rough for me and my mom. You see, my parents got a divorce when I was fifteen. It was hard for me, but my mom was more devastated. My parents had a love like no other. They met back in high school and fell for each other at a party. My mom is African American and my dad is White. You could imagine how that relationship might have been for them, but they made it work. My mom decided to leave the state for college while my dad stayed closer to home. They stayed friends all through college. Somehow "love" brought them back together. They got married and had my older sister and brother back to back. A few years later, I was born. My childhood was a good one. They seemed so happy and madly in love. I always wanted that…to be so in love that people wanted it too. Then it happened. I was fourteen and heard something downstairs, so I went to see what it was. I stood on the stairs and saw my dad at the door. I called out to him. He never turned around or said anything back. I asked him where he was going. No word. He picked up his luggage and walked out of the house. To this day, I can't stand him.

My mom placed my waffles in front of me. I ate them and drank my orange juice. When I finished, my mom cleaned up my plate.

"Mom, you didn't have to clean up for me," I said as I headed to the door.

"I know I didn't, but I want you to have a great day at school today," my mom said as she looked at me. "Promise me you will try your best to have an awesome day." I looked at her and smiled.

"I'll try, Mom." She smiled and kissed me on the cheek. After giving her one last hug, I headed out the door and got in my car, a Honda Accord. I put my key in the ignition. *Let's make my last year in high school a good one.* I thought as I reversed and headed off to school.

9:00am-Franklin High School

I pulled into my parking space and turned off the ignition. Grabbing my bag from the passenger seat, I got out of my car. Once out of my car, I saw my best friend, Sam MacArthur. She has long, dark brown hair, tan skin, and gray/green eyes. She is a little shorter than me since I am 5'6, and she is 5'4. Sam is a very interesting girl. She is energetic, gullible, optimistic, clumsy, and a ball full of fun.

The fact that she is a very optimistic person, she tends to see the good in people, especially guys who are probably not that great.

"Hey, Al-pal," Sam said as she hugged me. She had this huge smile on her face. I hadn't seen her since mid-July because I spent the remainder of my summer in Europe with my dad. "How was Europe?"

"It was nice," I said with a laugh. "I mean; I did have to spend it with Katie."

"Oh God. That must have been rough."

"I know." We both laughed. It was nice having my best friend back in my life.

"I'm pretty jealous because I was here talking to boys that lead nowhere," Sam said with a laugh. I looked at her and she knew she had mentioned the two words I hated the most: *Talking* and *Boys*.

"Sorry, Aly. My bad," Sam said with a laugh. We started to walk to campus when all of a sudden, a motorcycle roared through the parking lot. We stopped and turned around. I looked and saw this guy parked next to my car.

"My, my, my! Who is that?" Sam asked. Her eyes were fixated while I rolled mine. He took off his helmet and ran his fingers through his curly brown hair. Sam started to lose balance and said, "Holy shit, he's beautiful." Sam wasn't the only one whose eyes were glued onto this guy.

I just didn't get it. Why do girls get gaga over a hot guy? I'm not saying I'm not attracted to the male species, but I find more satisfaction in reading than a shirtless boy.

Sam walked over to the guy and said, "Hi, my name is Sam." She had this huge smile on her face. I joined her to make sure she didn't make a fool of herself.

"Hi," the guy said with a smile on his face. "My name is Ethan Price. It's nice to meet you. I just moved here last week."

"Well, welcome to Franklin," Sam said. "I could give you a mini tour before class starts." I realized this was my chance to get out before Sam asked me to help out.

"Hey, I have to run. Nice meeting you, Ethan," I said as I turned around and headed to campus. Sam called out my name, but I just kept walking. A grin appeared on my face as I took on my first day of senior year.

9:35am- Creative Writing

I walked into my first class of the day: Creative Writing. My schedule was great. I started my day out with Creative Writing, then Lit, Math, Lunch, and AP Psychology. After that class, I leave campus for the rest of the day, since I have taken all my science and elective classes. It's pretty nice, too, since most of my friends stay until three forty-five, and I go home at two forty-five. I put my headphones in and listen to music since class didn't start for another ten minutes. I pulled out my journal and read over what I had written this past summer. The good thing about going abroad was being able to find cool places to sit down and write about the location before anyone was awake to realize you were gone.

I looked at my phone and saw that Sam texted me. I was pretty sure it was about Ethan, so I ignored it. Mr. Smith walked in and class began. He welcomed us back to school and talked for a few minutes until someone knocked on the door. He went to open it. I was still reading my journal entries until the girls started whispering about something. I looked at the door and saw the Ethan guy I just met earlier. I heard all the comments about how hot he was and how people wanted a piece of him. It made me want to vomit.

"Hi, my name is Ethan Price, and I think that I'm in this class?" Ethan said as he showed Mr. Smith his schedule.

"You are," Mr. Smith said. He looked around to see if there was a free seat. "You can take your seat next to Ms. Pisano."

"Okay," Ethan smiled and walked over to the seat next to me.

Mr. Smith explained how everyone's seats are assigned for the whole school year, unless you need a new seat for a serious reason.

Great… I'm next to this guy for the next nine months. I thought to myself. I snapped back to reality and listened to what Mr. Smith was saying.

"So, class, to kick off the year, your first assignment will be due Friday. You will be writing a story using the descriptions of the person next to you to do so. This assignment is to get an idea of your writing skills and if they have improved from last year."

I rolled my eyes because I could not care less about this guy. I was more curious about how he got into this class if he was new to the area since Creative Writing isn't offered in a lot of schools in Washington, let alone in the nation. Ethan waved his hand in front of my face to get my attention. *Ugh…spaced out too long.* I looked at him and he had this smile on his face.

"Yes?" I asked.

"Hey, did you hear what Mr. Smith said?" Ethan asked still with a smile. "It seemed like you were in your own world."

"I wasn't in my own world," I rolled my eyes. "I tend to space out sometimes."

"Okay, if you say so," He laughed. "Do you want to get each other's descriptions, so we will be able to work on this later?"

"Sure," I moved my journal back in front of me. Ethan looked over at it.

"I like your journal. I like how it has WRITE right in the middle. Like a reminder," Ethan laughed.

"Yeah, I guess. Thanks."

I didn't get this guy. Ethan pulled his journal out and put it on the table while he looked for a pencil in his bag. I looked at his journal. *Coffee stains and worn out pages.* It looked like that journal had been through all kinds of crap.

"Wow, your journal is unique," I commented.

Ethan laughed. "Thanks, I take pride in it."

"Okay, let's get started. I'll go first."

"Cool beans." Ethan had a smile on his face.

"My name is Aly Pisano. I'm seventeen years old. I'm 5'6. My favorite colors are blue and black. I was born in Seattle. My favorite genre of music is indie/alternative, but sometimes I listen to G-eazy and Blackbear. I have been to ten concerts so far. I like fashion, but writing is more of my passion. My best friend is Sam. Ummm… I'm not that interesting, so that's me." I laughed.

"Well, I think you are kind of interesting," Ethan joked with a smile. "I'll go. My name is Ethan Price. I have been to ten different schools since I was twelve. I moved here from Portland. I'm seventeen too. I'm 5'10. My favorite color is green. I was born in Arizona. My favorite genre of music is indie too. My all time favorite band is Phoenix. I have seen them in concert three times. I like my motorcycle a lot, but my Nissan Maxima is nice, as well. And writing is my escape from this world for a little bit."

"Interesting." The bell rang and I put my stuff back in my bag. I started to head for the door.

"Bye," Ethan said as he waved to me. I was confused, so I kept walking out of the room and headed to my next class. I got to my next class and sat at my desk. My mind started thinking about this Ethan guy. Eventually, I focused back on the lesson.

12:45pm-Lunch

Once the bell rang, I headed to where I was going to meet Sam. I was pretty happy to find out we had lunch together and happier to figure out the rest of our crew did too. We walked into the senior lounge. It's basically a cafeteria that only seniors can eat in. It's a lot nicer than the regular lunchroom with the underclassmen. That's because every year the senior class improves it as their gift back to Franklin. I have to say, it is one of the perks of going to Franklin. Mason and Jake were sitting at a table when we arrived. Mason smiled and waved to us.

Mason Evans was the nicest guy you would ever meet. He was seventeen, 5'10, has faire, tan skin, and had these beautiful brown eyes. My favorite thing about him was his hair. He took a lot of pride in his curly brown hair since the curls were unique. They weren't just curly in specific areas of his hair. His whole hair was curly. Some people always told him to cut it when he was little, but he liked it and decided to keep it. Now, it's his best feature.

"Hey guys," Mason said as he bit into a sandwich.

"Hey Mas," Sam said with a smile as she sat down. "How's it going?"

"Sam… you talk so loud," Jake blurted as he rolled his eyes.

Jake Miller was a funny, faire skin guy. He was the same age as me, but his birthday was in September, mine was in October, so we would both be seventeen for a short amount time together. Jake was kind of the class clown in our grade. Everyone loved him. It's because he was a very outgoing, funny, chill and easygoing person. People were drawn to him. Most of them are girls, but he knows a lot of guys and girls. Sam looked at Jake and laughed. I sat next to Mason and Sam was on my left, which was across from Jake.

"Jake, I have missed you," Sam announced with a smile. Jake shrugged his shoulders and started to eat his lunch. "Anyway, guys...I love my classes. You guys know I always get a crappy schedule, but I guess Franklin realized how awesome I am and wanted to say sorry by giving me the best schedule ever."

Jake stopped eating and looked at Sam confused. "That makes no sense, Sammy. It's not like the school is out to get you. They make schedules randomly, dummy." He nibbled on his sandwich again. Sam started to pout and looked straight at Jake. "Look, if you want to go, I'm ready to take you down."

Mason and I laughed. As much as Sam and Jake bumped heads, they actually were really good friends. One time, Sam was heartbroken over a guy, so Jake came over to keep her company. After that day, their friendship grew stronger and stronger every day. I was starving, so I dug into my lunch.

"Hey, where's Brandon?" Jake asked.

"Oh yeah, I forgot to tell you guys," Mason said as he put down his drink onto the table. "He's helping out Ethan Price before they come to lunch." I started to choke on my sandwich. Mason patted my back. I caught my breath, Mason asked, "Are you okay, Aly?"

"Yeah," I said as I inhaled and exhaled for a moment. I swear that name will be the death of me.

"Now that you're okay, I'll explain," Mason said. "You see, Ethan is in our second period Math and third period English. After Mr. Hall finished his English lesson, we asked Ethan about what lunch period he had. He told us fourth. I explained to him how we and a few friends of ours had fourth, too, and I asked him if he wanted to sit with us." He drank more of his blue Powerade.

"He asked Brandon for directions to his next class, so once class was released they left and I came here." Mason's phone vibrated. He had a text message from Brandon saying they were on their way back here.

"Great, I can't get away from this guy," I thought in my head, but smiled on the outside. "Cool." A few minutes passed before Brandon and Ethan strolled into the senior lounge. Mason waved to them and they came over. I knew Ethan couldn't recognize me from behind— at least that's what I thought, until I heard laughing and looked in front of me. Ethan had a smile on his face and looked straight at me. He sat down in front of me.

"Hey," He said with that stupid smile on his face.

I looked over and saw Mason was confused. "Do you guys know each other?"

"Yeah," Ethan laughed. "We have Creative Writing together, first period."

Mason looked at me and laughed. "That must be interesting."

"So far, it has been cool. I think it's going to be fun, don't you Aly?" He looked at me with a grin.

I didn't understand this guy, but I went along with it. "Yeah, so much fun."

We spent the rest of lunch talking, eating, and most of all laughing at Sam's dumb jokes.

AP Psych: 1:45pm

After the bell rang, I headed to my last class for the day: AP Psychology. I was excited to finally take this class. A few friends of mine last year took it and said it was a difficult class, but so worth taking. I walked into class and sat in the middle. My headphones were in, so I couldn't hear anything. I pulled a book out of my bag and read a bit since class hadn't started yet. Out of nowhere, I felt a pat on my shoulder. Looking up from my book, Ethan was standing in front of me. I took out my headphones.

"Hey, is this seat next to you open?" Ethan asked. He was still wearing that stupid smile of his. I couldn't understand how anyone could be so happy. Then I realized something: if someone's life was good, then why would there be a reason to be sad? I couldn't be mean to him because one, he hadn't done anything to me and two, he wasn't that bad of a person.

"Nope."

"Cool, I'll take it."

He sat down. "You know; you must think I'm stalking you since we have three classes together."

"I wouldn't be surprised if you were." He smirked at me. Before he could offer a comeback, Mr. Hill walked in and began class.

2:45pm

Sam and I both leave at two forty-five every day. Sam had a class at a college nearby at 3:15, so she had to leave early. I, on the other hand, got to go home and sleep every day. We walked to my car. When we reached it, we saw Ethan on his bike. Sam smiled and asked, "Do you have early release, too?" Ethan looked over at us and smiled.

"Yeah, I finished all my other credits last year at my old school."

Sam whispered over to me, "Smart and cute."

I rolled my eyes and looked back at Ethan and saw him looking and smirking at me. I was confused and raised a brow.

"What?"

"Oh, nothing," Ethan said as he started his bike. "I'll see you guys tomorrow." He put his helmet on and drove off. Sam leaned and put her back against my car.

"You know; Ethan was the topic of conversation in most of my classes. It makes sense, that kid is hot."

I didn't understand why this Ethan guy was a catch. He's nice and good-looking, but is that all that matters to people? I realized the female population isn't like me, when it comes to relationships.

Sam started to laugh. "Oops, I forgot who I was talking to."

I nudged her off my car, laughed, and said bye to her. As she walked off to her car, I got in mine and drove home.

When I reached my driveway and parked, I looked at the clock in my car and saw it was three. Grabbing my bag from the passenger seat, I got out of my car. I closed the door and realized people moved into the house next to us. I was surprised to see that the house had finally sold. The people who lived in the house before were the Glenn's. They moved to California, but their house had been up for sale for the past six months and now someone finally bought it. I locked my doors and headed into my house. My mom wasn't home, so I went into the kitchen and made a cup of tea. Then went up to my room and changed into something casual, leggings and a big t-shirt. I sat at my desk and opened my MacBook Air. I decided to start the Creative Writing assignment now before I took my nap. Thirty minutes passed and I was halfway done with my story.

I closed my laptop, walked over to my bed, and took the well-deserved nap I earned for making it through my first day of senior year.

5:00pm

I woke up and rubbed my eyes. Throwing my sheets off, I decided to go downstairs. My mom was in the kitchen. I yawned and walked passed her to the teakettle.

"Hey sleepyhead," my mom said. "How was your nap?"

"Much-needed," I replied as I made tea. "How was work?"

"Tiring. I started in the new department, but I'm getting the hang of it." She got a bottle of water from the fridge. "How was school?"

"Interesting. Did you know people moved next door?"

"Yeah, there were moving trucks around the house when you were gone, so you never saw."

I put the kettle on the stove until it started boiling. When it was ready, I poured it into my mug and dropped in a few ice cubes. I preferred chilled chai tea. My mom was leaving the kitchen, but suddenly stopped.

"Your father texted me. He wants you to call to chat about your day later."

I said nothing. My mom knew I didn't like speaking about my dad, unless it was an important issue. I didn't answer her. I drank all my tea, put the mug in the sink, and headed up to my room.

"I'm going to go for a run before dinner."

"Aly."

I didn't turn around. I went to my room, changed, and left the house. I put my headphones in and started to run. As I passed by the house that was just sold, I thought I saw Ethan in the window, walking by. I realized I was going crazy, so I turned up the music and ran for three miles. After reaching the main road, I started to run back. When I was a few blocks away from my house, I started to walk, so I could catch my breath.

I passed by the house that was sold again and saw someone coming out. I couldn't see the person's face since they were throwing something in the trash, but knew it was a guy. When he turned around, it was Ethan. Not sure of what to do, I hid behind a huge bush dividing his house from the other. Footsteps got closer and closer, but then they stopped. Someone called his name, and he turned around and headed back into his house. I exhaled, ran back to my house, and closed the door behind me.

"How was your run, Aly?" I heard my mom ask from the kitchen.

I was still shocked that Ethan was my neighbor.

"Good, I'm going to freshen up."

I went up to my room and took a quick shower. I put on my set of PJs my mom got for me. Before going downstairs again, I looked out my window. Looking across, I saw it was a guy's room. Before I knew it, a shirtless Ethan was in my view. I turned around, hoping he hadn't seen me looking over. Then went back downstairs to eat dinner with my mom. After we finished, she cleaned up all the plates. I was about to head back up to my room when she said, "Don't forget to call your dad Al." I didn't turn around. I rolled my eyes because why did I have to call him, when he could have stayed and heard for himself. Then I remember:

People don't need to tell you they're leaving you. They can just up and leave. No note, no number, no address, they just leave. And that's life.

"I don't feel like calling him right now, but when I do, I will."

I went back to my room and closed the door. I fell onto my bed. I picked up my phone and saw I had five missed calls from my dad. I wasn't going to call him tonight, so I texted him for thirty minutes and told him about my day. After he said good night to me, I put my phone away, picked up my journal, and wrote how my day went.

"First day of Senior year.

Today was a good day. I feel senior year is going to be crazy since everything is changing and nothing is constant. My classes this year are great, plus I get to see my friends every day for an hour. We have new neighbors and Ethan is one of them. For some reason, I get this weird feeling about him. It is not some lovey dovey feeling but it's this weird feeling. Maybe I'm thinking about it too much, but other than that I'm ready for what this year has in store for me.

I put my journal on my bedside table and turned off the light. I put my covers over me and fell into deep slumber.

Tuesday: 9:00am

I got to school early and waited for Sam to walk over to my car. While I was waiting, Ethan pulled into his parking space. I rolled my eyes and tried not to pay attention to him. He held his helmet in hand. He walked past me, but then stopped. He turned around and smirked at me. I was confused why he was looking at me.

"Hey, neighbor," He said. "Did you enjoy what you saw in the window?"

He turned around and headed to campus. I looked straight at him.

I didn't understand how he knew, but I knew one thing:

Ethan and I had a lot in store this school year.

Two

A Week Later – Tuesday: 9:45am

It had been a week since school started, and my workload was piling up. After Ethan found out we were neighbors, I saw him every time I left my house. It sucked. He always had that dumb smile on his face and always said, "Hey, neighbor, how's it going?" In my head, I'd say, *"Pretty good, until you spoke to me."* But on the outside, I'd smile and say, "Alright." Then continue getting into my car and leave. The guy was always cheerful and I didn't understand it. Shaking my head, my eyes focused back onto Mr. Smith explaining the next project we were going to do in Creative Writing. This project would be year long and was called the Reflection Project.

"This project requires you to submit a reflection every eighth day of the month. You may print them and hand them into me or send it via email," Mr. Smith said. "Length isn't that important since it's your own reflection, but one is due each month. Then, from March until May, you guys will present what you have learned from this past year. This is why the monthly reflections are important: come February, you won't remember what happened in September."

"Now, the final summary will be focused on what you have learned this past year overall. I hope most of you will present because this assignment is a big grade. Your paper will be counted as half of the final exam and your presentation is the second half. But if you don't want to present in front of the class, that's okay. You will just have to do it before or after school. Any questions?"

I was pretty eager about this project since I heard how interesting it is at the end of the year. During the time of presentations, the students in Creative Writing are excused from their last two periods of class, since they spend the remaining afternoon in the auditorium, presenting their reflections. After Mr. Smith finished answering questions, he gave us time to work on our stories, since they were due tomorrow. I pulled out my laptop, plugged in my headphones, and worked on my story. Listening to music helped keep me focused. Then someone patted my shoulder. Ethan smiled. I took my headphones out of my ear.

"How's it going?"

I looked at him with a confused face, because I didn't understand why he was asking. He realized I was confused a bit and started laughing.

"What?"

"Ohhh, nothing." He smiled.

Still puzzled how he figured out we were neighbors, I asked him.

"How did you know I was your neighbor?"

Ethan laughed. "It's pretty funny. When I was going to throw trash away, I saw a Honda Accord and it had all these stickers on the back of it. I figured it was a girl's car. Then, while I was changing, I saw a girl looking into my room. I couldn't see her face since she turned around quickly, but I knew a girl lived in the house across from me. When I got to school and saw the stickers on the back of your car, I knew whoever got out of the car was my neighbor. You got out and you were the Peeping Tom looking into my room." He smirked a bit. "So your stickers gave it away."

I rolled my eyes. "Lots of people have stickers on the back of their car."

Ethan nodded. "That's true. Oh yeah, and I saw you get into the car that morning too, so that gave it all away." He smiled and laughed again. I didn't know whether to tell this guy off or to put on a fake smile and move on with life.

"Besides, it's cool having you as a neighbor."

He moved closer to me and whispered, "Since I basically see you walk around your room all the time."

I looked straight at him. "What?"

He had this huge grin on his face. "I mean, our rooms are right across from each other, so I have a clean view into your room." I turned back to my laptop and put my headphones back in because I couldn't keep listening to him. A few minute later, Katie Marsh came over to talk to Ethan. This girl was bent over with her ass sticking out. Katie Marsh was the typical popular spoiled rich bitch of high school. Oh, I forgot to mention that we are step-sisters.

I minded my business because Katie was the last person I wanted to go at it with. *Too early in the morning and too much on my mind as well.* My mind started to drift off and I thought about how I hadn't looked across to see how much I could see in Ethan's room. I also think I didn't want to check, so it didn't seem creepy. I looked back over at Katie and saw her being her usual self when it comes to guys. Twisting her hair. Biting her lip. Touching his hand. Ethan didn't seem to realize it because he was looking straight at her. He had that dumb smile of his on his face.

"I'm sorry you have to sit next to Aly, Ethan," Katie said as she twisted her hair. "It must be rough." I knew she was saying that so I'd react someway.

Ethan laughed and said, "What's there to be sorry about? It's actually a lot of fun. Since I get to learn more about my neighbor." I hit him on the arm. I didn't want girls finding out we were neighbors because then people would get the wrong idea.

"Oh my, that's even worse," Katie said with a shocked face.

"Well, at least, I'm not you," I said softly.

"What?" Katie asked.

I grinned. "Oh, nothing."

"Whatever." Katie turned around and headed back to her seat.

"Bye, Ethan." We glared at each other as she walked back to her seat.

"Why is there so much tension between the two of you?" Ethan asked confused.

"Well, it's normal to have tension between step-sisters. You see, Katie doesn't like me, so it's different." I said.

Ethan was shocked. "You guys are step-sisters?"

I laughed. "Yeah, most of our grade was shocked, too, when they saw pictures of us together on her social media. Trust me, it was miserable taking any picture with her."

"Do you guys live together?"

I laughed so hard when he asked me that. "Hell no! She lives with my dad and I live with my mom. If we lived together, I would probably die."

"Is she that bad?" He laughed.

"I mean, not to the male species, but for some reason, her goal in life is to make my life hell. We have gone to the same school since I moved to Washington, but we never talked. Once her mom got engaged to my dad, she started making my life hell. I still don't understand why or what I did to her, but I'm pretty sure I never will."

I spaced out a bit and Ethan asked me a question, but I didn't hear him.

"What? Sorry."

"So your parents are divorced?

"Yeah." I put my laptop away since the bell was about to ring.

Ethan smiled. "Same here, and that's one thing we have in common."

I rolled my eyes a bit, but I had a grin on my face. "If you say so."

The bell rang. As I left Creative Writing, I waved bye to Ethan. This made him happy because his face lighted up with a huge smile. He was about to wave bye back, but a bunch of girls crowded around him. I shrugged my shoulders and headed out of the class. Giggling a bit, I headed to English. As I walked into class, Preston Chase was one of the few people in the classroom. He said, "Ew," as I walked by. I rolled my eyes and went to my desk.

Preston Chase was your typical popular boy, who lived in the rich part of the suburbs. He was 5'10, had brown hair, faire skin and a fit body since he played on the soccer team for our school. I couldn't stand him. He was just one of those guys who seemed nice, but in reality, he was a douche. When I found out we had English and Math together this year, I wanted to puke.

Cara walked into class and sat next to me. Cara Smart was a funny girl. We became friends during sophomore year since we had History together. This was our first class together since then.

"Hey, Aly," Cara said when she was in her seat. She had a smile on her face, and I smiled back. All of a sudden, Conner Abel walked into class. Conner was that kid in your class who you wished wasn't in your class. Conner, for some reason, loved trying to talk with Cara. She rolled her eyes when she saw him walk into the classroom.

"Cara! Look, it's your boyfriend," Preston said with a smirk. By this time, everyone was in the classroom.

"Shut up, Preston," Cara said with a sigh. Preston looked over to me and smirked. I was confused about why the hell he was looking at me. Mrs. Sheppard walked into class and started the lesson for today. While she talked, I started to think about Preston and why I can't stand guys like him. Guys who dressed like the typical high school boy who acted like they are the shit. Then I realized something: I can't stand the male species in general, or at least, the ones in high school.

Lunch: 12:45pm

It's lunchtime, and Sam started talking about life.

"Guys, life is good."

"Are you high or something?" Jake asked as he finished taking a bite out of his sandwich.

"No… why do you always think that?"

"Sam… you don't make sense sometimes."

"You aren't sense."

"What the hell does that mean?" Jake had this confused face.

Mason and I started laughing. We both think Sam and Jake should date, but they try hard to put a barrier in between them. Sam rolled her eyes at Jake and pouted. "You're an ass."

"Nah... I'm pretty rad."

Mason and I looked at each other and laughed. We've had been friends since I moved to Washington, and he was the first one to welcome me when I arrived at the middle school. Since that day, we have been best friends. I forgot Ethan was across from me until I turned my head and saw him looking straight at me. We looked straight at each other, until Mason made a comment.

"Why are you guys looking at each other like that?"

Ethan smiled and said, "It's okay since we are neighbors." I was drinking water, so when he said that, I started to choke on it. Mason patted my back and looked concern. "Are you okay?"

Once I got my breath back, I said, "Yeah. Water went down the wrong pipe." I looked at Ethan and he looked worried.

"Next time, don't say things like that when I'm drinking water, ass."

Ethan laughed. "You're so silly." He had that dumb smile on his face again.

"It's true, though, Ethan," Mason said. "Aly gets very clumsy when you say something out of the blue. One time, we were eating ice cream and I told her I was going out of town for a week. She somehow started choking on it." He started to laugh.

"I was 12 and childish."

"Yeah, but it's pretty funny because who chokes on ice cream?" Everyone at the table started to laugh. At first, I pouted, but I later joined in with them. My eyes glanced over to Ethan and he was looking at me again. He had a smile on his face. It was a smile different from the ones he usually has. I was a bit confused about why, but then he looked away, so I forgot about it.

2:45pm

My favorite part about school was the fact I got to come home at two forty-five every day. It gave me more time to take a full hour nap and still had time to get ready for work. My job is at a local bookstore in the area and oh how I love working there. The building is like a library --- always filled with books. Once I got into my room, I did my normal routine: Drop my stuff on the ground and jump onto my bed. I looked at the ceiling and slowly closed my eyes. When I closed my eyes, I started to remember something from my past. *I saw him.*

After opening my eyes, I decided not to take a nap.

I made my way to my desk where the pile of homework awaited to get done before work. My printed schedule was on the upper left side of my desk. *Tuesday and Thursday: 5:00-10:00pm* was what it said. I began with finishing my Creative Writing assignment. Thirty minutes passed and the assignment was completed. I looked at my bullet journal. *AP Psych reading due Friday.* So I began reading. Once the clock hit four, my homework went back into my backpack since work was at five.

My normal work attire was American Eagle jeggings and a blue t-shirt. Then I did my normal work routine: Go to my bathroom and brush my teeth again, look in the mirror and make sure my hair was okay, then leave my bathroom and pass by my window. Only glancing over for a minute, I saw Ethan was in his room and he had no shirt on. Quickly, I turned around so he wouldn't see me and vice versa. Grabbing my purse, I headed downstairs. Once in the kitchen, I warmed up leftover pasta and ate it at the countertop. The door unlocked and my mom walked into the house.

"Hey." She put her bags down and walked over to the kitchen.

"Hey." I continued to eat.

"You have work today, don't you?"

"Yeah, I should be home around ten."

"Okay, have a good day at work." She hugged me before she went upstairs to change. Once finished, I looked at my phone and saw that it was four forty-five. Grabbing my keys and purse, I headed out the door. Once in my car, I backed out and drove off to work.

Arriving at four fifty, I walked into the bookstore and said hello to my boss, Mr. Thomas. Mr. Thomas was one of my mom's friends. He gave me the job when I was fifteen since his son was leaving for college in the fall. I took it since it helped take my mind off of the divorce.

"Hello, Aly," He said back with a smile. I smiled back while putting my stuff in the back. Once done, I returned to the front.

"How's business so far?"

"It's pretty good since college students are coming here to get textbooks for a reasonable cost."

"Do you think this evening is going to be busy?"

"Probably not, since it's a Tuesday and most of the students came in earlier in the day."

"Well, that's good for us."

"It is. Here's a list of things I need you to do."

Looking at the list, I saw there were only a few things that needed to be done. Smiling, I said, "Okay, I'll get on it." I walked away from him and got to work.

7:00pm

I finished the first five things on the list, so I sat down and rested for a bit. The door opened and someone walked in. Hearing Mr. Thomas sound pleased to see whoever it was, I walked back to the front to see who it was. I looked and saw Matt. I walked over to him and hugged him tightly. He hugged me back. "Hey, Al-Pal." Matt Thomas was Mr. Thomas's son. When I first started working here, Matt trained me. Matt was a senior while I was a sophomore. He was very nice and funny. Working with Matt was something I enjoyed back then. When we were both scheduled together, his dad trusted us to run the store alone whenever he had to step out a bit.

"Son, why are you here tonight?" Mr. Thomas asked. Matt goes to school in Downtown Seattle, which is about a two-hour drive from the town we lived in.

"Well, you know how I was interning this past summer, well I got back yesterday. I thought I would surprise my family, with me being back home," Matt said with a smile. "And since I don't start classes for another week, I said, 'What the heck?'"

Mr. Thomas hugged his son. Seeing how happy he was to have him back in town warmed my heart a lot.

"Aly, is there any way you could watch the front while we catch up in the back? You can finish the rest of the list Thursday."

"Sure." I smiled and sat at the cash register. They walked to the back of the store. An hour passed and the store was still pretty slow, so I pulled out my phone and texted Mason and Sam. The door opened and I said, "Welcome!" I wasn't paying attention because I was looking at my phone. That was until I heard the person's voice.

"Hey, neighbor."

I looked up and saw Ethan standing right in front of me. He started to laugh.

"Now, I know where you work," He said. "This place kind of fits you: it's weird."

I was about to roll my eyes, but then I raised my eyebrow. "Did Mason tell you I work here?"

Ethan started to laugh. "No, but I did ask him where some bookstores in town are, and he told me about this one." I rolled my eyes and realized Mason was going to get it. Ethan smiled.

"What can I help you with?"

"Do you guys sell any Stephen King's books?" I was surprised that he reads.

"Yeah, we do. I'll show you where they are" I walked over to where Stephen King's books were. Ethan followed me and he looked to see which ones he wanted. As I walked back to the cash register, Matt came back out to check up on me.

"Hey, is everything good out here?"

"Yeah." I smiled at him. It was nice having a great friend back.

"So you started school, right?"

"Yeah, sadly." I had this huge smile on my face while talking with Matt. This is probably because back when I started Sam said I had the hots for him and she said that I "wanted a piece of that." I covered my ears when Sam said it. The smile might have formed because back then, we accidently kissed in the back. I was running to the back to get some books and he was heading to the front. As I was going down a step stool, I started to lose balance. Matt caught me in his arms.

"You okay?"

"Yeah." I put a piece of hair behind my ear and looked down.

"You should reward me with something."

So I thought about it and decided to kiss him as a reward. I was shocked that I was kissing him, but then he kissed back. I stopped it and realized where I was. He headed back to the front and I got what I came for. I don't think I'll ever forget that kiss because it was my first. That always was also before everything in my life went to shit. Matt started laughing at me since I spaced out.

"You haven't changed a bit, Al-Pal. How is your mom?"

"She's good. Dating again, actually!"

"That's great!" Matt had a smile on his face. He put his hand on mine. This triggered flashbacks of *him*, so I moved my hand away from his. As I turned, I saw Ethan coming over with three books in his hand. I wasn't sure if he saw, so I smiled and said, "Is that all?"

"Yep." He smiled back.

"Hi, I'm Matt," Matt said.

"Hi, I'm Ethan." He had a smile on his face.

"Well, Al-Pal, I'll let you work." He turned around and walked to the back of the store.

"Is that your boyfriend?"

I looked straight at Ethan. I knew he saw the hand grab.

"No…I don't have a boyfriend."

Ethan laughed. "Oh, you guys seemed to be close so I thought he was. Plus, he's good looking."

I laughed. "Well, I'm not interested in him. We have been friends for the past two years, so we're close."

"Oh, that makes sense." Ethan laughed. He passed me the books, so I could check him out. I gave him the bag after he paid.

"Thanks, I'll see you tomorrow." He smiled and waved goodbye. I waved back while watching him walk out the store. Turning around, I put my back against the cash register. I started to realize something: Ethan wasn't so bad. I looked at my phone and saw it was nine.

I walked away from the cash register, locked the door, and started closing for the bookstore.

THREE

I woke up to the sound of pouring rain. That was one of the things that happened often in Washington. Some people saw that as a curse, but I saw it as a blessing. I lay there listening to the rain hit against my window and eventually got out of my bed and headed over to my desk. I looked at the calendar and saw that I finished the first week of September. It was the best feeling. School had been taking over my life since it started, even though I take only five classes. The classes are pretty demanding, but I've been managing. Tonight was finally going to be an "R&R" night with my friends, which I deserved.

Being a high school senior was stressful enough, but then put the college application process on top of that and I'm basically screwed. Since I wasn't meeting my friends until late, I decided to start on a few applications. I was applying to five schools: Iowa State, University of Southern Cal, Pace, University of Washington-Seattle, and University of Portland. My dad went to the University of Southern California, so there was a high chance of me being accepted, at least, that's what my dad thought. I hoped to double major in Communication and Creative writing with a minor in Marketing.

Writing is a key factor influencing who I am today and I don't know where I would be without it. When my mom got me a journal at the age of twelve, I got hooked. My mom always told me, "My daughter is going to be a beautiful author." Since that day, it has been my goal. I don't think I have to be a best-selling author, but to just know people read my work would be an amazing feeling. I hoped to publish a book before I turn thirty. I mean, I am seventeen right now and thirty seems far away, but it will be here before I even know it. I looked back at the screen and started working on my college apps.

After I finished two applications, I decided to get ready for the day. It had been a week since the last time I washed my hair, and it was getting greasy. Once I finished my shower, I wrapped myself in a towel and walked over to the sink to wash my face with face wash. After I left the bathroom and went back to my room, I put on a huge t-shirt since I was going to work on my hair for the next hour. Having naturally curly hair, thanks to my mom, always took a long process of combing, blow drying, and straightening to style it into my normal look.

An hour passed. Looking at myself in the bathroom mirror and smiled--I was proud of what I saw. I unplugged my straightener and turned off the bathroom light. Then walking over to my dresser, I decided to wear black leggings and a loose t-shirt. After closing my dresser, I froze in place. Remembering how my dresser was right in front of my window, which meant Ethan had a clear view of me, if I started changing. I moved out of his line of vision and started to change. Being the only one in the house, since my mom worked on Saturdays, I made breakfast for one. I put on some music while cooking and started dancing around the kitchen. Past memories started to come back to me: how when my siblings were living at home, we always had fun cooking Saturday morning since it only was the three of us at home. Closing my eyes and opening them up again, I continued cooking.

2:45pm

Most of the day was spent in my room. After finishing my AP Psych homework, I decided to work on the August reflection that was due on Monday. A few minutes passed, when all of a sudden, there was a knock at the door. Opening the door, I saw my older brother, Nick, standing, with a smile on his face.

"Hey, Al-man," he said. I felt so much happiness and hugged him tightly. "Someone missed me huh?" He messed up my hair a bit, but I didn't care, because my brother was home. I think he knew what I was thinking because he looked down at me.

"It's good to see you too, sis!" He came inside and I closed the door.

"Is mom home?" We made our way to the living room. Nick sat down on the couch.

"No, she'll be home around three."

"Okay, cool."

I was a bit confused about why Nick was here. "Why are you here, Nick?"

"I wanted to surprise mom." He had this smile on his face.

Nick goes to college in California, and my older sister, Hollie goes to the University of Washington. I had seen my sister a few times since she left, but I hadn't seen Nick for the past two years. Actually, the last Christmas we had--- when my parents were together--- was the last time I saw him. Now, we would just video chat during the holidays since he couldn't afford the travel expenses for his trips home. He also didn't want to come home and deal with the tension from the divorce. When Nick hit my shoulder a bit, I realized the amount of time I had spaced out.

"You still space out like crazy." He laughed.

I laughed. "Yeah. I have missed you a lot, Nick." I put my head on his shoulder.

"Yeah, I missed you a lot too Al." He smiled and decided we should play video games until mom got home. At three, I heard the door unlock.

"Aly, where are you?" My mom asked.

"In the living room," I said.

"You are never going to believe the d-" My mom froze in place once she looked up and saw Nick on the couch. Nick paused the game and got up and walked over to her.

"Hey, Mom!"

She looked at him and hugged him tightly. It was nice to watch because I saw how happy my mom was to see Nick. Even if it was for a little while, it didn't feel so empty in the house anymore.

6:45pm

I headed over to Mason's house since the whole gang was hanging out at his house tonight. When I got to the door, Mason opened it and smiled.

"Hey, Al," Mason said. "Come in." Mason took my stuff and placed it on hooks next to the door.

"Do you need anything before we go downstairs to the basement?" He asked.

"A bottle of water would be nice."

"Make sure you don't choke on it." He laughed. I rolled my eyes and we walked over to the fridge. Mason's mom was in the kitchen cleaning plates.

"Hello, Mrs. Evans," I said with a smile.

"Hello, Aly. You look beautiful more and more every day," She said with a smile.

"Thank you!"

"Mason, can I order the pizza now?" She asked him.

"Yeah, you can now, Mom. Thanks." He smiled and passed me the water bottle. She smiled and walked away.

"Was I the last person?"

Mason laughed. "Yeah."

"Makes sense. You have to save the best for last."

We both laughed. Mason hit my arm lightly. "If you say so." We headed down to the basement. Once we got there, I saw that Brandon was playing Uncharted. I ran over and sat down next to him. "Which one are you playing?"

"Second one," Brandon said, still focused on the game.

I always loved video games. It's probably because when Nick was at home I would watch him play. Once he left for college, he passed down his PlayStation 3. Now, I play video games whenever I get the chance. Sam started to laugh about something. I looked at her and then around the room until my eyes saw Ethan talking with Mason. I turned back around and continued to watch Brandon play the game. Ethan came over and sat across from me.

"Hey neighbor," he said with that gleeful smile of his. I tried not to pay him any attention.

"Shit! I have to pee. Beat this level for me, Al," Brandon said. He went to the bathroom and I took his seat, Ethan moved and sat next to me with this smirk on his face.

"You can't ignore me, you know that right, neighbor."

"I wasn't ignoring you. I'm focused on the game."

Ethan rolled his eyes. "Yeah, right." Even though I wasn't focused on what he was talking about, he started to get on the topic of his dad. "My dad met your mom and said she is very nice."

I was still focused on the game and said, "Cool."

"He also said we are having dinner with you guys tomorrow night."

I paused the game and looked at him. "What?"

"Yeah, he told me this morning. I said the same thing." I never remembered my mom saying we were having dinner with Ethan's family, but then it came back to me. She told me last night, but I was focused on something else, so I zoned out while she was talking. Looking back at the game, I knew Ethan had that cheerful smile on his face again.

"Well, I'm excited to have dinner with your family tomorrow too." Ethan laughed.

He put his arm around my shoulder and started to bring me closer. This triggered a flashback and I started to tense up since the last person to do something like that was *him*. I dropped the controller.

"Stop!" I yelled. Everyone looked at me since I was standing up now and yelling at Ethan. Ethan looked confused. I realized what I just did.

"I'm sorry." I turned around and ran upstairs.

"Aly! Wait!" Mason said as he ran after me. I ran up to Mason's room because I didn't want to make a scene in front of his parents. I walked into his room and closed the door. I sat on the floor on the left side of his bed and put my head down on my knees. A few minutes passed and I heard a knock on the door.

"Aly, can I come in?" Mason asked with a worried tone in his voice.

"Yeah." The door opened and Mason walked in. He closed it behind him. He walked over and sat next to me. "What happened, Aly?"

"It's nothing." I didn't look at him.

"Is it about *him*?"

      I stared at Mason. He knew I meant *him*. One day, we were hanging out in Mason's room and decided to play truth or dare. We decided to take it up a notch and grabbed a bottle of booze. Every dare you chickened out of you took a shot and every truth you didn't tell; you took a shot. The game started to get interesting since I was the only one drinking. I got pretty wasted, to the point where I started asking Mason what he thought of me. He was taken back because he saw a very different side of me. I kissed him, and the kissed started to get deeper until Mason pushed me away.

"I can't do this," He said.

"I don't get it. Why doesn't anyone want me? Not my dad, not you, or even him."

I started to cry and Mason moved over to comfort me.

"I loved him, Mason, so why would he do what he did to me? H-he took off my clothes, even though I told him no." Mason didn't know who he was, but he realized what happened. After that day, Mason had always been there for me when things triggered flashbacks like when a guy put his shoulder or put his hand on top of me.

"Yeah. When Ethan put his arm on my shoulder, it triggered a flashback." I started to feel tears run down my cheek. Mason wiped them away with his thumb. "It's going to be okay." He helped me up and took me to his bathroom to clean up a bit before we headed back to the basement.

9:00pm

      The night ended and I headed home. Once I parked my car, I

saw Ethan pull up a few minutes later. I got out of my car and walked over to him. He rubbed the back of his head and was a bit confused about what was going on.

"Hey, I'm sorry for how I acted," I said. I knew I couldn't fully explain to Ethan why I acted the way I did. I smiled and hoped he would forgive me.

He smiled back. "Okay, I forgive you, neighbor."

"Okay, good. Good night." I turned around and headed into my house.

Next Week-Wednesday: School-10:15am

I walked into Creative Writing class. It seemed that everyone was talking about Katie Marsh's Fall Party happening this Saturday. Katie had, for the past two years, thrown a party in the fall. This is because for one weekend every September, my dad and her mom go out of town for the weekend. Katie invited anyone she knew, or, at least, knew of, to come. The party, I heard, was always epic, and that's why everyone made it such a big deal. I mean, I could care less about if I got invited, but I'm pretty sure Katie made it her mission for me not to attend. Probably because I would then have leverage over her and she couldn't let that happen. I started working on the assignment that is due next week. We had to write a three-to-four-page love story that could end beautifully or horribly.

"I'm sure Aly is going to write a horrible ending since she is so heartless," Katie said with a laugh.

"At least, mine isn't going to be as predictable as yours," I shot back at her. Katie flipped her hair and turned around. Ethan laughed a bit. I looked over at him and smiled. Things between Ethan and I seem to be good since last Saturday. After Mr. Smith was done teaching today's lesson, we were supposed to spend the rest of class working on today's assignment. I focused on the assignment until Katie and her clan of dummies came over with an invitation. She looked at me and laughed. "This isn't for you, Al." Then she looked at Ethan and gave it to him. "It's for him. I think it would be awesome for you to come, Ethan. Plus, you can bring a guest with you."

"Yeah, it would be great for you to meet the other guys from our class," Penny said with a smile on her face.

"And girls," Daniela said with a smirk on her face. I rolled my eyes and my stomach felt sick. Meet Penny Mayfield and Daniela Maxwell. I had a class with them last year and they seemed to be pretty nice people, but then I found out they were Katie's minions and complete idiots.

"You know, Katie," Ethan said with a smile, "I'll come if you won't protest who I bring." Katie's eyes were dead set on him.

Katie flipped her hair and said, "Of course, not." I started to drink my water while they were talking because maybe it could drown out Katie's desperation.

"Okay, then I'll have to take my neighbor right here," Ethan said with this huge smile on his face. When I realized what he said, the water went down the wrong pipe again. It literally felt like I was drowning. Katie started laughing along with her minions. Ethan patted my back just like Mason had at lunch. After I got my breath back, he asked, "Are you okay, neighbor?"

"Yes." He looked at me with a smile. "So will you go with me?" This time he was smiling so hard I wanted to hit him in the face so he would stop. It felt like every girl's eyes were on me and that they were wondering why he was taking this Plain Jane girl with him to this year's party. I thought about it for a while and decided what the hell.

"Yeah, I guess I'll go with you."

Ethan smiled and his eyes were on me. He had these beautiful hazel eyes that had a way of drawing you in. Or at least, that's what it felt when I was looking at them. I saw Katie roll her eyes.

"Are you sure you're going to be free this Saturday?"

I looked straight at Katie and knew she was pissed off, so I smirked and said, "Hell yeah, I will. Can't wait to see you!" She walked back to her desk and her minions followed. I heard giggling and looked over at Ethan. I raised an eyebrow and said, "What?"

"It's funny how she reacted like that," He said with a laugh.

I smiled. "It's nice to see her realize she has been defeated."

We both started laughing and got back on task with our assignment.

Saturday: 5:45pm

I couldn't believe I was actually going to a high school party. I got out of bed and started to get ready since Ethan and I were carpooling. I decided to wear my American Eagle dark washed jeggings, a V-neck t-shirt, and a denim jacket. I looked at myself in the mirror. Then went over to my jewelry box and put on these blue earrings and a matching necklace. After I took one last look at myself in the mirror, I grabbed my purse and headed downstairs. John and my mom were sitting on the couch. John Griffin was my mom's boyfriend. He was forty-four years old and had tan skin. He was five-eleven and had brown eyes and hair. He was a nice, silly, humorous, smart guy, and made my mom really happy, so I was happy.

"Hey, I'm about to go leave for Sam's," I said as I put on my shoes.

"What time will you be back?" My mom asked.

"Probably around ten forty-five. Eleven at the latest."

"Okay, be safe." She kissed me goodbye on the forehead.

"Okay. Bye, mom. Bye, John." I waved goodbye to them and walked out the door. I walked over to Ethan's driveway and saw him standing next to a car. I was surprised because he was always riding his motorcycle. I heard laughter and looked at Ethan.

"Are you surprised I have a car, too?" Ethan asked with a smile. "We live in Washington, neighbor. If it rains a lot or it's cold, I can't ride my bike."

"Oh, that makes sense," I said with a laugh. We got in the car and headed over to the party.

We parked at Sam's house and walked down to Katie's house since it wasn't too far away. I remembered when my dad moved into this house when we came back from Europe. Once we walked up to the porch, I heard the music inside and the scent of weed in the area. We walked into the house. A real high school party isn't like the ones in movies. The movies keep it clean; a realistic high school party was disgusting. This is because people were making out with each other or drunk out of their minds and acting like fools. Ethan looked at me with a grin.

"High school parties are the best." He gave me two thumbs up. I started to laugh. Katie came over and welcomed Ethan. I didn't really care, but her outfit caught my eye. It was this tight black dress that made everything---and I mean *everything*---pop out at you.

"Have a good time! Drinks are in the kitchen and living room." She smiled and walked over to greet the next guest. I rolled my eyes. *People pleaser.*

"I see Sam and the gang," Ethan said. I looked over in the same direction and saw Sam, Mason, Jake, and Jenn all hanging out together. We walked over to them. Sam was so happy to see me and hugged me tightly. The scent of alcohol was all over her and I knew she was gone.

"Hey, guys," Jake said as he sipped his beer. "Welcome to the party of the year."

"WOOOOOOO!" Sam yelled.

"How drunk is she?" I asked Jake.

"She had three cups of the fruit punch, but I think someone spiked it with something strong. I saw Penny put something in it and walk away."

Sam started to dance to the music. Sam was a good dancer when she was sober, but when she was really drunk, she was a hot mess. I started to laugh. Ethan looked at me and asked, "Do you want something to drink?" I looked at him and smiled. "No, I'm good."

"Okay, I'll be right back." He walked over to get a drink. Sam started to dance, so Jake and Jenn headed off to help her. Mason and I started to laugh.

"Will you be okay alone?" Mason asked.

"Yeah, I'll be alright."

Mason smiled and walked off to help them. I stood there and looked at my phone. All of a sudden, I felt someone's presence there, so I looked up to see Preston standing in front of me. I looked back at my phone, hoping he would get the hint.

"Hey-there, sexy," He said in a drunk tone. I realized he was drunk and his friends, on the other side of the room, were cheering him on. Before I said anything to him, Ethan came to my rescue.

"She's with me, buddy," He said with a smile.

He laughed and drunkenly said, "Whatever." He walked back over to his friends.

"Thanks," I said to Ethan.

"No problem."

"What are you drinking?"

"Water." He laughed.

I was surprised. "Why?"

"Well, I'm driving us home and I don't want to drive under the influence, neighbor." He had that gleeful smile on his face that made me want to punch him, but I realized this guy was pretty smart.

Three hours passed and I looked at my phone. It was ten thirty-five. I drank one cup of fruit punch. Jake was right: that punch was spiked. I walked around looking for Ethan. He was talking with a few other guys from school, but then my view got blocked. Katie came over and started laughing with her clan of dummies.

She whispered in my ear. "Ethan will be mine." Pushing her aside, I headed over to Ethan. "I need to head home."

"Okay."

He said bye to his friends and we headed out the door. Katie said bye to Ethan, too, and she gave him a hug. While hugging him bye, she kissed him on the cheek and looked straight at me. "I'm sorry," Katie said once they stopped hugging.

"It's cool. Thanks for inviting me to the party." He smiled and walked out of the house. Once he was out the door, Katie smirked at me.

"Hope Dad doesn't find out about this. Night, Katie!" I walked out of the house with a huge smile on my face. We walked down the sidewalk. I knew the alcohol was in my system because it finally started hitting me as I kept walking. I started to losing my balance and laugh uncontrollably. Ethan held onto me since I was stumbling. "Why are you laughing?"

"I find it funny how this is the first time in a long time I have to rely on a guy," I laughed through the alcohol. I remembered why I don't drink in public. Ethan had this confused look. "What do you mean?"

"Well, I don't believe in relationships or dating. At least in high school. High school relationships are bullshit anyway because how can you 'love' someone so much you want to be will them forever. Like, that's crazy. High school is four years of your life, so why worry about dating now?" I was drunk, but serious. "Besides, love is a controllable feeling. People say love is this unexplainable feeling, but that doesn't make any sense to me. People fall in and out of love pretty quickly, so I think it's a controllable emotion. Nope, I know it is. I witnessed it with my parents. High-school sweethearts. Thought to be together forever, but people were wrong."

Ethan stopped walking. I realized it and let go of him. He looked at me and realized I was serious about everything I just said. I was confused about why since I said the truth. I was about to ask him if he was alright, but then the confused face went away and his smile returned. We walked the rest of the way in silence.

11:00pm

We got back to Ethan's house and I got out of the car.

"Is it cool if I walk you to your door, neighbor?" He asked with a smile.

"Sure, why not?" I smiled back. Once we got to the door, I looked at him. "Thanks for the ride and helping me out back there." Ethan had a smile on his face.

"No problem." We stood there looking at each other. I was about to head in, but then I heard Ethan say something, but didn't hear him well.

"What?" I looked at him.

"I will change your view on love," Ethan said casually and with a smile. He turned around and headed back to his house. I was confused as hell, but headed into my house. I locked the door and walked over to the living room. John and my mom were sleeping on the couch. After putting a blanket on them, I headed up to my room. Then I closed my window and changed into my pjs, which were a big t-shirt and shorts, since it was hot. Once dressed, I fell onto my bed and looked up at the ceiling.

I started to reflect on what Ethan said until I fell into deep slumber.

FOUR

October

Saturday: 9:00am

    My alarm went off and I slowly made my way out of bed. Walking over to my mirror, I looked at myself. *Ugh, the face of a high school senior.* My window was in the background and I decided to move the curtains aside. I looked into Ethan's room to see if he moved his curtains too. While looking over, Ethan moved his curtains aside. He waved at me and had a smile on his face. Rolling my eyes, I waved back. I turned away from my window and looked around my room. There were tons of clothes and stuff on the ground, so I decided to spend the morning cleaning my room a bit. Once my joggers were on, the work began.

    Two hours passed as I lay down on my floor. You don't realize how dirty a room can get after a few weeks have passed. I decided to connect my Beats Pill and listen to music while cleaning. Once connected, a song started to play. The song was Lizatomania by Phoenix came on. While picking up my clothes from the floor and putting them on my bed, I danced in place. Even though I sucked at dancing, I went with it since the song was my favorite. While spinning around, I ended up in front of my window and saw Ethan. He was standing there laughing. I opened my window.

"What are you laughing about?" I asked.

He opened his window. "Thanks for the good entertainment." He held his mug up to me and then took a sip.

Dang, he looked good. I thought to myself. He had long pants on and no shirt, so I saw how fit Ethan kept himself. It was an interesting sight. I rolled my eyes, closed my window, and turned around. Ethan was probably smiling that gleeful smile of his. For some odd reason, that put a grin on my face as I continued cleaning my filthy room.

Monday: Lunch

I got lunch off campus since I forgot mine this morning, so I was the last person at the table. Arriving at the table, I saw them talking about something that seemed important. Jake saw me and called out to me. "Look who's finally back." I walked over with a smirk on my face and said, "Was I missed?"

"Of course," Sam said.

I sat down. "So what are you guys talking about?"

"We were talking about our fall break plans," Mason said. "Ethan was telling us how he wants to go to Portland that week."

I was surprised because I hadn't been to Portland since we moved from there five years ago. Ethan took a sip of his water and then put it down.

"I moved around a lot when my parents were together, but when I was twelve my parents settled in Portland, so it kind of was my hometown."

"Really?" Mason said. "Aly moved from Portland when she was around twelve too." I hit him in the arm because I knew what he was trying to do. Ethan laughed a bit.

"You should take Aly with you since it's her hometown too," Jake said with a laugh.

"That's a great idea," Sam said. "Aly is always in town during fall break."

I rolled my eyes. "I have fun here during that week." The whole table started to laugh because they knew that was a lie. Ethan looked at me and had this smile on his face.

"So will you go with me, neighbor?" Ethan asked.

"Ummmmm... No." I rolled my eyes and headed to the bathroom. Ethan got up as well and said he had to use the bathroom too. He caught up to me and whispered to me. "At least, think about it." I looked at him and gave in. "Okay, I'll think about it." A huge smile appeared on his face as he turned around and headed back to the table. Realizing he wasn't actually going to use the bathroom at all, he just wanted time to talk with me about it, I turned around and headed to the bathroom with a grin on my face.

Saturday: 8:00am

I woke up and realized what day it was: Dad's day. I wondered if closing my eyes would make the day pass. If I had it my way, I wouldn't spend any time with a man who walked out on his family, but the court thought it would be best if I spend every second and last Saturday of the month with this man. It was miserable at the beginning because he would pick me up early in the mornings before I saw my mom. That changed, once I got my license, so my mornings could be spent with my mom. She always took off work those days, so we could have breakfast together before I left.

Realizing there was no getting out of it, I got out of bed and started to get ready for the day. I decided to keep it casual and went with a T-shirt and jeans. Once dressed, I packed a few clothes for the weekend. Knowing we were probably going out for dinner tonight, I brought a dress, a pair of leggings, jeggings, and threw in two loose t-shirts. After my bag was packed, I grabbed my purse, and keys, and headed downstairs. John and my mom were cooking breakfast once I walked in. A smile appeared on my face since I was so happy to see my mom happy again. She turned around and smiled.

"Good morning, Al," She said as she hugged me.

"Good morning, mom." I hugged her back. "Hey, John."

He smiled back. "Morning, Al."

I sat at the countertop. "What are you making?"

"My famous pancakes and turkey bacon," John said.

My mom laughed and looked at him. "Who said they were famous?"

He looked back at her and had a grin on his face. "Oh, this really beautiful woman."

My mom raised her eyebrow. "Oh really?"

"Yeah."

They moved closer and kissed. A laugh came out of me because it was funny how cheesy they were. My mom turned and looked at me. "Are you ready to go to your dad's house?" I rolled my eyes. "I'll never be ready to go."

"I'll take that as a yes."

John finished making breakfast and the three of us ate together. Thirty minutes passed and we finished eating. My mom followed behind me and we hugged one last time. She kissed me on my forehead.

"Will you be okay?" I asked.

"Yeah, I think I will." She looked at John with a smile.

"Be safe." I smirked.

My mom looked back at me with a shocked face and then we both laughed. I opened the door and headed to my car. Then I put all my stuff in my trunk and got in the driver seat. I backed out and drove to my dad's house.

When I arrived at my dad's house, I realized this was my first time being here in the day time. The house looked different from how it did three weeks ago since it was daylight and there were not a bunch of horny teenagers everywhere. The house probably isn't what you think a millionaire man would live in. The color of the house was blue and had white columns in front of the door. The landscape was beautiful. Since it's Fall, nothing was blooming and breathtaking, but when it's Spring time and the flowers are blooming, it would be breathtaking. I pulled into the driveway and saw Katie's car, knowing this weekend was going to suck. I went to the door and put my bags down. When Katie opened the door, we looked at each other with disgust.

"Oh... it's you."

"I'm not excited to see you either." I rolled my eyes. Katie's mom, Tracy, came over and asked who it was. When she saw it was me, she came out and hugged me. Her hug was tight. She let me go and brought me in. Katie rolled her eyes after she closed the door and headed back upstairs. As I walked in, the inside of the house was massive. When first walking in, there was a larger staircase that stood in front of the doorway, leading you to the six bedrooms and six bathrooms upstairs. To the left, there was a dining room, capable of seating up to twelve guests. To the right was my dad's study room. I don't really know what was in there because he kept the doors closed. Being the CEO of a company required a lot of organization, so he kept his things private (unless we need to use the printer).

"Your father went to play golf with a few buddies," Tracy said. "He will be back soon."

I smiled at her. "Okay." She asked me to come into the kitchen with her, so I followed. We talked about stuff for a little while I was still in shock from the inside of the house.

"How are the twins?" When I asked that, they came down the stairs. They saw me standing there and attacked me with hugs.

"Breakfast is ready, Sarah and Samantha," Tracy said. They sat down at the table and got ready to eat. "Aly, you can go upstairs and set up your room if you want.

"Okay." I smiled and headed up to my room. My face was shocked when I stepped in. The room looked just like the room I had back in my dad's old house. The tapestry was on the wall and painted the same creamy white color. Tracy knocked on the door. "I forgot to tell you where your room was, but you found it."

I turned around. "Did my dad do this?"

"Yeah, he wanted you to feel at home whenever you came over, so he decided to recreate the room you had back at the old house." I was surprised. "I'm taking the twins to a play date and going to the grocery store. Is there anything you need?"

"I'll text you my list."

"Okay, I'll be back soon." Tracy walked out of my room and closed the door behind her. Then I put my bags down and walked around the room. What I liked most about the room was the view of the sunset in the back. Plus, there was a balcony looking over the backyard. While lying on my bed and looking at the ceiling, I was surprised my dad went through all that trouble to recreate my room. While thinking, my eyes started to drift off and I fell asleep.

3:00pm

Waking up to the sound of my phone going off, I reached over and answered. "Hello," I said.

"Hey neighbor," Ethan said on the other line.

"What do you want?"

"Where are you neighbor?"

"I'm at my dad's house for the weekend."

"Ewww, that must suck."

I laughed. "Yeah, it's been alright so far." Katie walked into my room. I was confused about why the wicked witch of the west had walked in.

"Who just walked in?'

"The last person I expected to walk in."

"Katie?"

"Yep."

"Well, don't do anything crazy." Ethan laughed on the other line.

I laughed too. "Okay, bye Ethan." I ended the call and put my phone back on my bedside table. Katie stared at me. I was confused why she was looking at me. "What can I help you with?" Katie started to laugh. "Ethan Price would never go for a girl like you, Aly." She started walking around my room. "Since you're a heartless person." I turned around. "Excuse me?"

"Aly, you have never publicly dated anyone let alone liked someone, so you must be some heartless loner." I had never let what Katie said about me get under my skin, but this time, it hit me. It's because I realized she wasn't lying. Katie grinned and got closer to me. "Aly, stay out of my way because Ethan will be mine." She walked out of my room high and proud. I lay back on my bed and started to think about Ethan as I fell back asleep.

5:30pm

I woke up and tried to get out of my bed, but couldn't. Confused why I couldn't get out, but then I saw Nathan. He started to touch my hair and then my face. Yelling, but no sound came out of my mouth. I closed my eyes. He whispered, "You're a heartless loner and no one could ever love you." I opened my eyes and looked around my room. I realized it was all a bad dream. My dad was sitting on the edge of my bed.

"Hey."

"Hi."

"Sorry, I came to wake you up from your nap since we are going out for dinner, but then you started tossing and turning in your sleep…and shouting."

"Sorry, I was having a bad dream. I don't want to talk about it." I got out of bed and went through my bag.

"Aly…are you sure?" He had this confused face.

"Yes…it was just a bad dream, okay."

"Okay… I'll let you get dressed." He got up and started to head to the door. "I'm trying Al, give me a chance."

He closed the door as he left. The way I acted was rude and he was trying, but I couldn't tell him about the dream. I pushed the dream to the side as I got dressed. When my outfit was on, I spun around the mirror. The dress was black with a red belt in the middle, which made my curves look great. My hair was put into a braid since I wanted it casual. My phone started to vibrate. I had a text message from Ethan.

"Hope you didn't kick Katie's ass too hard."

"Nah, not worth my time."

He texted back fast. *"Good thinking !☺"*

I smiled as I headed out of my bedroom for dinner.

Sunday 3:00pm

I finally got home and fell right into my bed. My mom went out to brunch with a few friends, so the chance of me seeing her wouldn't be until later. The clothes I wore at my dad's house got put into my laundry bin. Then I headed up to my roof, so my focus would only be on my September reflection that was due tomorrow. I heard someone call out "Hey neighbor, what are you doing up there?" Looking down, Ethan was standing there. "Hey, the view up here is amazing."

"Sure."

"If you don't believe me, come on up. The door is unlocked, so come on."

Ethan smiled and came on up.

Ethan made it up to the roof and sat next to me. "You weren't lying about this view." I laughed.

"I love how this place is my getaway place. When my parents were arguing about something, I would come up here and everything faded away. Plus, the sunset is beautiful up here too." I was looking out while explaining this to him. Turning my head, I looked at Ethan. He was smiling at me. I was confused why he was smiling at me.

"That's really interesting," Ethan said. "I think everyone should have a getaway place."

"What's yours?"

"I think Portland is mine. I was always happy there and whenever I was sad, I always knew a place to go and rest my mind."

I got a text from my mom saying she was on her way home, so I told Ethan we had to go inside before she got back. He laughed. "Okay." We went back into my room.

"Your room is very different from what I see in the window." He started to laugh because he saw this crazy girl dancing horribly in this room. I rolled my eyes.

"You roll your eyes a lot," Ethan said. I laughed, knowing that I did roll my eyes a lot. "It's probably because of stupid people or hearing stupid things." I lay down on my floor and looked up at the ceiling. "Can I ask you a question?"

"What's up, neighbor?" He asked as he sat down next to me.

"Do you see me as a heartless loner?"

Ethan was confused. "No, you seem like a really caring person. Why do you say that?"

"Katie called me that last night after I got off the phone with you."

"I see you as this girl who wants to go places and you don't think that a guy needs to be involved in that right now," He said looking at me. "I don't think there is anything wrong with that. You shouldn't let what Katie said get to you." As my eyes looked at him, a grin appeared on my face. This caused me to answer his question about Portland.

"So about this road trip you are going on," I said.

He looked at me and smiled. "Neighbor, it's okay if you don't really want to go."

I looked at him. "Silly boy, I guess I could go with you."

This shocked look appeared on his face. "Are you sure?"

I wasn't sure what was in store for our friendship, but I decided to take a leap.

"Yes."

FIVE

Thursday before Fall Break: 11:45am

As I was leaving math, Preston walked up to me. I was confused why he was walking next to me. He looked at me and rubbed the back of his head.

"Hey, I'm sorry for how I acted at Katie's party."

I stopped walking and looked at him. He didn't make eye contact with me.

"I was drunk and didn't remember much from that night until a few days ago and I wanted to apologize." He walked away.

Still confused, I was glad he apologized. It showed he wasn't that bad of a guy. I continued walking to the senior lounge and saw only Sam and Jenn at our table.

"Hey, all the guys went to get lunch off campus," Sam said with a smile. "They will be back soon."

"Oh okay, cool," I said as I sat down next to her.

"Do you wish Ethan was here, Al?" Sam asked with a laugh. I started eating my lunch and realized Sam was just being Sam.

"Did you know, Jenn, that Aly is going with Ethan to Portland?" Sam asked. "It's going to be so cute." Jenn was surprised. "Is that true, Aly?"

"Yeah," I said. "I was going to tell everyone today."

"It's going to be so cute, Al," Sam said. "You guys will fall in love. I know you don't believe in that kind of stuff, but you can't go on a road trip with a hottie like him and not fall for him. It's going to happen. You are going to go to Portland, have the time of your life, and then somewhere along the way, you will fall in love with him."

"Sam," I said.

"What if he makes you realize that love isn't all that bad? Then I can finally tell my best friend everything about relationships and stuff. Holy shit, Aly he could be your first!"

"SAM!" I said with an angry tone. Sam thought I was a virgin, but I wasn't. Sam stopped talking. She realized she went too far.

"Look…we are just friends. We aren't going to fall for each other. We aren't going to fall in love. And I'm sure as hell not sleeping with him." I turned back around and ate my lunch. I knew I upset Sam when she didn't say anything. The guys returned and asked what they missed. Jenn told them nothing, but Sam's face was blank until Jake made a joke about her and she went back to normal.

"So guys, Aly decided to go to Portland with me," Ethan said.

Mason smiled. "That's awesome."

Jake started laughing. "Finally, she's getting out of her element." I rolled my eyes at him. We all started to laugh and talked about other stuff.

3:00pm

Ethan and I hung out in my kitchen after school. "We need to make a plan how we are going to tell our parents," I said as I finished baking my brownies.

Ethan sat on my countertop. "I don't understand why we have to when it's just a trip."

"I don't know if my mom will let me and a boy, who are both

teenagers, go alone on this."

Ethan started to laugh as he ate a brownie.

"I didn't make them for you," I said. Ethan smiled and ate one anyway. I rolled my eyes. As I bit into my brownie, I came up with a plan.

"Invite your dad for dinner at my house tonight. We will cook them dinner and talk with both of them at the same time."

Ethan smiled and said, "That's a brilliant idea, neighbor." He pulled out his phone and texted his dad to come over for dinner. He texted back saying "okay ☺". I looked at Ethan and asked him, "What does your dad like?"

"His favorite food is pasta," Ethan said.

"Pasta it is," I said.

"I'll help you out." I laughed.

"You know how to cook?"

Ethan smirked.

"Yeah, I love food. Why wouldn't I know how to cook?"

I laughed and we started cooking dinner…together.

6:30pm

I was getting dressed for dinner and decided to wear this dark blue tie dye dress. It had pockets. Looking at how the dress fit on me in my mirror, I unbraided my hair and fingered through it. A smile appeared on my face as I looked at my appearance in the mirror. Once I got downstairs, Ethan was standing in the kitchen.

"Everyone is waiting in the dining room," Ethan said. When he turned around, this shocked look appeared on his face when he saw my dress.

I put a piece of my hair behind my ear. "What?" I could tell he was flustered since his faire white cheek turned bright red. "Nothing." I laughed. "I'll move some of the food into the dining room."

"Hello," I said to my mom and Ethan's dad. They smiled at me and my mom asked, "What's going on?"

"We are making dinner tonight."

They looked at each other and smiled. Once back into the kitchen, Ethan finished making the pasta sauce. We headed back into the dining room with the sauce in a bowl.

Thirty minutes passed and we finished eating. I cleaned up the plates and got dessert. When I walked back into the dining room, Ethan was talking with our parents about the trip. I gave each person a brownie on a smaller plate. Ethan's dad took one bite and was in heaven. "So dad, you remember how I asked to go to Portland over the break with a friend?" Ethan asked.

"Yeah," Ethan's dad said.

"Well, that friend would be my neighbor next to me."

"Really?" My mom said.

"Yeah," I said.

"You guys aren't dating, right?" Ethan's dad asked.

"No." Ethan laughed. I blushed a bit because I knew this would happen.

"Why is your face red, Aly?" My mom asked. *Mom! Why would you point that out?!?!* I thought to myself. Ethan looked at me and laughed a little.

"I don't know how I feel about that," Ethan's dad said as he finished his brownie. "Can you give us a few minutes to talk about it in private?"

Ethan and I took the plates away and went back into the kitchen. My palm felt sweaty since the waiting was killing me.

"Have faith," Ethan said. "It will work out in the end." Ethan smiled at me. I decided to have faith as well. A few minutes passed, so we walked back into the dining room and sat down.

"So we talked about it and we have a decision," Ethan's dad said. There was a pause until Ethan asked, "What's the decision?"

My mom grinned. "We have decided yes, as long as you guys update us through text or call."

"And there are two beds in the room," Ethan's dad said.

I got out of my seat and went over to hug my mom. "Thank you so much, dad," Ethan said. "And thank you, Mrs. Caulfield." He grabbed my hand and we headed over to the living room. He looked at me and hugged me. Then he spun me around.

"WE ARE GOING TO PORTLAND, ALY."

I was shocked because this was the first time he had said my name and not neighbor. I smiled hugely. "Yeah, we are."

Ethan and his dad left after our parents discussed the trip a little more. When I went up to my room, I looked at the clock and saw that it was eight. After changing into a big t-shirt and shorts, I fell onto my bed and looked up at my ceiling. I smiled. I was excited for the adventure that was about to happen in the next few days.

SIX

Saturday Night: 8:00pm

   Tonight was a treat myself night, playing my favorite game series, Uncharted. Mason came over, so we could hang out before I left for Portland tomorrow. Mason sat in my computer chair and watched me play. "Are you excited for the trip tomorrow?"

"Yeah," I said. But on the inside, I was really excited for the whole week in Portland.

"That's good. I'm glad you're getting out of the town for a little while."

I laughed. "Yeah. Plus, I haven't been to Portland in so long." I handed the controller to Mason, so I could start packing.

Mason smiled and then looked at me. "Is there anything going on between you two?" I looked at him and started to laugh because Ethan and I were just friends. And only friends. Mason smirked and laughed as well. "I'm kidding, you know that right?" I laughed. "Yeah."

"But do enjoy your time there, Al. Try to forget about everything back here, except me of course." I smiled and hugged Mason.

"Thanks for being my best friend Mas." He looked at me and smiled.

"That's' what I'm here for."

Sunday: 8:45am

I woke up and rubbed my eyes. I reached for my phone and saw a text message from Ethan. *TODAY IS THE DAY! I REPEAT TODAY IS THE DAY!* I laughed and got out of bed. As I got ready for the trip, my mind started to think about the last road trip I went on. It was with Sam and Mason. We went to a beach three hours away. A smile appeared on my face because those were the good memories I cherished. After getting dressed, I gathered my stuff and headed downstairs. I saw Ethan and his dad at the countertop as I walked into the kitchen.

"Good morning, neighbor," Ethan said with that gleeful smile I hated. I walked over and sat down next to him. My mom made waffles since they were my favorite. She put a plate in front of Ethan and I. Ethan's dad and my mom went into the dining room to eat, so we had space. I remembered how Ethan said that he had a little sister.

"Where's your little sister?" I asked as I cut my waffles.

"She's at a friend's house," Ethan said as he ate a piece of his waffles. "Sleepover last night."

"Oh, okay." I laughed a bit.

"Yeahh, she's Miss Popular."

"So are you dude." I hit his shoulder.

"Nooo, I'm not. I'm just friendly." Ethan laughed and ate more of his waffles. "And everyone loves you." I ate a piece of my blueberry waffles. "I'm pretty sure you don't. I mean you are mean to me all the time." Ethan grinned. I rolled my eyes and realized Ethan was an idiot. "You're an idiot. We're friends now obviously, so it's natural to make fun of each other." Ethan's face lit up. "We're friends!?!" "I hate you…" I cut my next waffle. Ethan looked over at my plate. "You have blueberry waffles!?!?! Can I have a piece?" He used his fork and took a piece. "Hey!" That stupid cheerful smile appeared on his face. "Thanks, Neighbor." His teeth were showing this time. I rolled my eyes and finished my breakfast.

By nine forty-five, Ethan and I finished packing his car with our bags in the back. Ethan drove a Nissan Maxima. It seemed like one of the newer models since it had an aux in it. We hugged our parents goodbye and headed off for this exciting adventure. Since Ethan was driving, I was in control of the aux.

"No JB or some shit like that," He said with his eyes on the road. I laughed. I was surprised he actually thought I listened to him. "Not every girl is a part of that fan club," I said. "That's what you think," Ethan said. "But every girl I have drove with puts him on and its death."

"What a typical boy." I laughed. "But, don't worry, we won't listen to that. I got a song." I went through my Spotify songs and decided to go with *Don't Stop* by Blackbear.

"I think I drank too much last night
Too much Grey Goose, better yet, champagne
Still afraid of goin' up too fast, slowin' down too soon"

This song was my go to dancing song, so I started jamming out in my seat. Ethan looked over at me for a second and started to laugh. I continued jamming out. When my eyes glimpsed over, Ethan was smiling. It was a different smile though. One I had never seen before. This caused me to smile too for some reason.

11:45am

I fell asleep, probably because I jammed out too hard. Rubbing my eyes, I looked outside, realizing we were at a rest stop. Ethan opened his door and realized I woke up. "Good afternoon, neighbor." He smiled at me. "Hey," I said. "How far are we now?"

"We are about to hit the Oregon border." Ethan smiled. "Well, what are we waiting for?! Let's head out!" He smirked and got back in the car.

We headed back on the road. I put on some music and looked out the window. I loved car rides for this reason: it was so relaxing watching everything pass by you. It was, even more, fun looking into other cars to see what they were doing. I loved the idea of car rides because we are all going somewhere. Every person. We are all trying to get to a destination and the journey is one hell of a ride. Especially when you go with another person. I looked at Ethan and smiled. He looked at me for a second and giggled a bit. "What?" I realized what I did and looked away. "Nothing." A smirk appeared on his face. "Don't fall for me now, okay?" I laughed. "Of course not." I got my jacket from the back, made it into a pillow and drifted back into a deep slumber.

12:45pm

An hour passed and Ethan woke me up. "We're here," He said as he shook my body. I rubbed my eyes and realized we had arrived at the hotel. We got our bags out of the trunk and put it in a luggage roller. We went into the hotel and checked into our room. Ethan signed everything and we headed up to our room, 505. After I put the room card in, Ethan dropped his stuff in front of the door and fell onto his bed. "Home sweet home." I laughed and rolled my eyes. "Weirdo." He looked up at me. "Neighbor, that's not very nice."

"Oh no! Holy shit! Did I hurt your feelings?"

Ethan rolled his eyes and realized I was being sarcastic. "Unpack, sassy neighbor." I laughed and started to unpack.

5:45pm

After we finished unpacking, Ethan took a nap. While he was sleeping, I walked around the hotel. When I came back, he woke up. We decided to head out. We left the hotel and walked down the street.

"It's great to be back home," Ethan said with a rested smile on his face. "Honestly, Portland is my home. I know where everything is, how to get around town, or where to get a good dessert if I wanted one. Since I have always moved around, nowhere ever felt like home. That was until I moved to Portland. When my parents got divorced, my mom moved to California and my dad stayed here. We lived in downtown, so I grew up here for two years until we moved out to the suburbs. Since my dad didn't want me to move to a different school again, he allowed me to continue going to my old high school, Lincoln. There I met my best friends and the people I trust the most today. We would always go to eat after school at a diner or hang out at the park across the street."

I was shocked how invested Ethan got when he talked about Portland. He laughed and looked at me. "Sorry for my rant about my love for this place, neighbor." I laughed. "It's okay. It's interesting."

"It is?" Ethan raised his eyebrow. "How?"

"Because it makes you happy," I said. "And it's interesting learning about other people's happiness."

Ethan smiled. "Yeah, if you look at it like that." He looked at his phone and then back at me. "You don't have to say yes, but my friends are at that diner I told you about, and I want to surprise them

69

that I'm back."

I saw that he wanted to see them a lot, so I smirked and said, "Why not?" He smiled and we continued walking to the diner.

6:00pm

When we got there, Ethan walked in front me, so I could follow behind him. As he walked in, a girl said his name in a shocked tone.

"Hey," Ethan said. The girl ran over and hugged him. Then kissed him on the cheek. I was shocked because I was right in front of them. Ethan laughed as the girl let go of him.

"Good to see you, Rachel," Ethan said with a smile on his face. "This is Aly." Rachel looked at me with a smile. "Hi Aly."

We walked over to the table Rachel was sitting at. The table said hi to Ethan and looked happy to see him. Some guy asked him, "What are you doing here?"

"I'm on Fall break now and wanted to come back for a week." Ethan smiled. Rachel smiled as well. "That's great. You can sit next to me." Before Ethan could say no, Rachel pulled him down into the seat. Rachel was beautiful. She had long brown, curly hair, tan skin, and a picturesque smile. Her style was perfect. She was wearing jeans, a t-shirt, and a flannel tied around her waist. She also was wearing these dark red Converse. That girl knew how to dress. I saw a seat available next to another girl down the table, so I sat next to her.

"Hi, my name is Casey," Casey said with a smile.

"Hi, I'm Aly," I said. Casey had short, light brown hair. It came a little bit past her shoulder. It was curled today from what I could tell. She had style too. She was wearing this dark blue dress that had straps. She had a cardigan on her chair as well, since it was a bit cold outside and black booties on. I looked over to Ethan and Rachel as they talked with one another. It was interesting seeing how well they were friends. Casey saw how engaged I was with them because she started to laugh. I looked at her confused. "What?"

"It's funny," Casey said. "Rachel and Ethan became best friends when he moved here back in middle school. Then sophomore year they started dating. They were the power couple at Lincoln and brought us all together as well."

All of a sudden, this guy named Finn, joined into our conversation. "The day they broke up was shocking."

"Ethan was so in love with Rachel, but then out of nowhere, she broke up with him," Finn said. "I think it's because she found out Ethan was moving before he got the chance to tell her."

I was confused because they still looked tight. Casey saw my confusion face and said, "They are still tight, but it's not like how it used to be."

"Plus Rachel is very touchy feely, so don't worry too much," Finn said.

I started laughing because I knew why he said that. They looked at me confused. "We are just friends," I said. They started to laugh. Now I was confused.

"I'm not sure I believe you because Ethan has looked over here a few times already," Finn said as he started to laugh again. I looked over at Ethan and he had that stupid delightful smile on his face. He looked over at me and we looked at each other. It was only for a few seconds, but for some weird reason, it felt like longer. I looked away and started talking with these new friends of mine.

8:40pm

After we parted ways with the others, we started walking back to the hotel. We walked for a little bit until Ethan broke the silence.

"What were you talking about with Finn and Casey?" Ethan asked.

I smirked because I knew he was nosey. "None of your business," I said as I looked at him. "They seem like really cool people, though." Ethan laughed.

"Yeah, they are. Finn and I have been friends for the past five years and Casey for the past four and a half years. Finn is very funny and Casey might seem conservative, but she's actually really fun and a goof ball at times. I became friends with them through Rachel, actually."

I started to laugh when he mentioned Rachel. "You two seem to be close." Ethan laughed and smiled.

"Well, we became friends when I first moved here and dated for two years."

"That's a long time."

"Yeah, I guess, but I'm glad to have her in my life still, though." Ethan smiled and I smiled back even if I honestly didn't want to. We continued walking and talking as we made our way back to the hotel.

Once back at the hotel, I put my back against my pillow and turned on the TV. "Can I take a shower first or do you want to go?" Ethan asked. "I'll wait," I said. Ethan went into the bathroom and closed the door. I texted my mom and told her we got here safely. Ten minutes passed and steam started coming out from the bathroom. I looked over and saw Ethan walk out of the bathroom with no shirt on and only a towel wrapped around his waist. I had seen Ethan shirtless from afar, but it was different when I was in the same room as him. He worked out. His abdomen had a six pack and had the formation of the V. My eyes were fascinated by his beautiful body and I couldn't control myself as my eyes kept moving down. That was until Ethan started calling my name.

"Neighbor," Ethan said with a puzzled look on his face. "Why are you staring at my body… and junk?" I started to get flustered. "Put a freaking shirt on." Ethan smirked and asked, "Am I making you uncomfortable since I don't have a shirt on?"

"Put a fucking shirt on." I threw a pillow at him.

He dodged the pillow and looked at me. "Hey! We wouldn't want me to let go of this towel would we?"

My ears were in shock from what I heard. I threw myself in my covers and looked at the wall. Ethan laughed.

"It's okay, I'll change into clothes in the bathroom."

I turned back around and saw that Ethan went back into the bathroom. I turned the TV back on and watched while in bed. Ethan came back out in a shirt and pants. I don't think I would have been okay if he just slept with only his pants on. My mind started to think about everything. Like how something was changing inside of me. This change felt scary because I knew what happened last time change like this happened to me. For some reason, though, when I looked over at Ethan on the other bed, this warm feeling filled up inside of me. He looked different now. He looked relaxed and calm. He looked over at me and smiled.

"Good night, neighbor." He turned off the TV.

"Good night, Ethan." I smiled back.

I turned back around and closed my eyes.

The smile was still on my face as I started to fall into a deep slumber.

SEVEN

Monday: 7:00am

I woke up and rubbed my eyes as I walked into the bathroom. As I turned on the shower head, the steam warmed up the room. This steam caused me to yawn and rub my eyes one more time. My clothes landed on the floor as I hopped into the shower. The water cascaded down my body and pooled to my feet. This caused me to stand there and ponder about my thoughts, until I heard a knock at the door.

"Hey neighbor, are you in there?" Ethan asked. *Obviously idiot.* I thought to myself because that was a stupid question, but then again Ethan asked dumb questions sometimes.

"Yeah, what do you need?" I asked. I heard laughing from the other side of the door. "Nothing, but if you need anything let me know." His footsteps got quieter and quieter as he walked away. A little confused, I shrugged my shoulders. After turning off the shower head, I pushed the shower curtains to the right and looked around for my towel. I realized why Ethan asked if I needed anything. Since Ethan took a shower first last night, I left both of my towels on my bed. My mind didn't think to check if they were in the shower this morning. Making my way to the door, I cracked it open a little. *I can't believe I have to do this.* I thought. *Ughh.*

"Hey Ethan, I need you," I said through the cracked door.

"Yes, neighbor?" Ethan asked as he walked to the cracked door. I stood on the left side of the door so Ethan couldn't see anything.

"I need my towels." Ethan started to giggle a bit. I was sure he had a stupid gleeful smile on his face.

"You mean the towels on your bed?"

"Yes, those towels." I was annoyed because he found so much entertainment from this.

"Okay, I'll get it for you." Ethan walked over to my bed and brought the towels to me. He passed them through the crack. Once he moved his hand, I closed the door. He started to laugh through the door as he walked back to his bed. I sighed and got ready for the day.

10:30am

We went down to the lobby and ate breakfast. As we were heading downstairs, Ethan stopped at the front desk and asked for something. When he came over to the lobby, he told me we were going to a museum today. When we finished breakfast, we headed for the museum. We waited at the bus-stop. We took a bus ride since it was a quicker form of transportation then walking. Plus, it wasn't too far from the hotel. It arrived and we got on. I took the window seat and Ethan sat next to me. I loved looking out the window as we drove pass the other cars. For some reason, joy filled up in me while watching everything passed by. It reminded me how nothing is constant in life. Ethan touched my shoulder to get my attention since I had been so invested in what was happening outside. I looked at him.

"We're here," He said. We got off the bus and the museum stood in front of us. The beauty of the exterior left me breathless. I decided to take a picture of the museum before we went inside. I stepped back to get the whole museum in view. I wasn't watching where I was backing up, and started to fall backwards into the road, since there was a curb. I thought I was going to fall and hit my head, so I closed my eyes and waited for the fall. I never fell. Ethan was in front of me as my eyes opened. He grabbed my hand and pulled me into his chest. I looked up at him, he had this worried look on his face. I was surprised how worried he was. "Are you okay?" He looked at me with these worried eyes. My face got flustered and I shyly said, "Yeah...thank you." He still had this serious look on his face. "You need to stop being so clumsy, Aly." I could tell he was scared. I looked at him. His frown went away and his cheerful smile came back on his face.

"Well, to make sure you're not clumsy again, I'm going to hold your hand." He entwined his hand with mine and we walked into the museum together. I thought it was a joke, so I went along with it.

4:00pm

After the museum, we decided to get lunch. We went to get pretzels at this bakery. Ethan got a salty pretzel and I got a cinnamon pretzel. We walked next to each other as we ate our pretzels. Ethan smiled at me.

"Did you have a good time at the museum, neighbor?"

I looked at him. "Yeah. It reminded me of the time I went with my dad."

Ethan seemed shocked. "Sorry."

I laughed. "No, you're fine. It brought back good memories with my dad." Ethan grinned. "Well, that's good, neighbor." We continued to walk back to the hotel.

Tuesday: 11:00am

I was sitting in my bed on my laptop working on some break homework. I seriously couldn't get away from school even if I tried. I looked over at Ethan and saw him on his phone. "Hey Ethan," I said. "What's the plan for today?" He looked over at me and smiled.

"I'm not sure yet," he said. Then his phone started to ring. He answered it and said, "Oh, hey Rach." I decided to brush my teeth, so Ethan could have some privacy. As I headed to the bathroom door, Ethan grabbed my hand. I turned around and looked at him. He mouthed the words *wait* with a smile. I decided to sit down on the edge of my bed and wait. Ethan finished talking with Rachel and hung up the phone.

"I have the plan for today." I looked at him and was a bit worried what he planned after talking with his ex/best friend. "What are we doing?"

"It's a surprise," Ethan said. "Let's go." He grabbed my hand and we headed off.

It was twelve clock when we arrived at a park. *Downtown Portland's Annual Street Fair* was stretched across a large sign above the park's gate. We walked in and as I looked around, I saw fields of trucks and vendors.

"What do you think?" Ethan asked with a smile on his face. "They do it every season, but each one has different trucks and vendors."

I loved it. People of all different sizes and shapes walked around the park. Everyone seemed to be there to try something new. The thought produced a huge smile on my face. Ethan messed up my hair. I glared at him. *What an ass.* I thought. He laughed because of the face I was making. "What's wrong neighbor?" *Your stupid self. Idiot.* I thought. I shrugged and kept walking and looking around. Ethan caught up with me. I stopped because I was confused by what he was looking at. "I see Rachel," He said. We started walking over to her.

"Hey Rach," Ethan said with a smile. She turned around and this huge smile appeared on her face. "Ethan! Hey!" She hugged him and he hugged back. I stood there feeling very awkward. She let go of him and looked over at me. She smiled and hugged me too. I was surprised. Why was this happy-go-lucky girl hugging me?

"Rachel, you might kill her if you keep hugging her," Finn said. He wasn't lying. The girl gave tight hugs. She let go and still had this joyful smile. "Hello, Aly." I smiled back. "Hey, Rachel." I looked past her and saw Finn and Casey sitting on a blanket on the ground.

"Is the whole gang here too?" Ethan asked them.

"Yeah, they are," Finn said. "But they're checking out the fair. Rachel said you were coming, so we were waiting for you guys to get here."

"And now you're here," Rachel said as she grabbed his arm. "I want to show you something." Ethan couldn't say anything before being whooshed away. I stood there as they faded into the crowd. A sigh came out of me for some reason. "Sit down, Aly," Casey said. I sat down in the middle of Finn and Casey. Finn said, "Sorry Al. I can call you Al, right?" I shook my head, confused why she was saying sorry.

"Rachel doesn't think about her actions sometimes," Casey said.

"More like all the time when it comes to guys," Finn said. Then he laughed. "When does Rachel ever think?" Casey started to laugh. I looked at them, confused why Casey was saying this.

"I have this feeling Rachel is trying to win back Ethan," Finn said once he stopped laughing.

"That would be crazy," Casey said with a laugh. "I mean; she broke up with him.

"Yeah, but there is a chance. Rachel said that Ethan and her applied to the same college so if they both get in and go, she wants him back in her life somehow. What better way then as her boyfriend or boy toy or something?"

I was shocked to hear that. Ethan did seem like the guy who would be in a committed relationship in college. I mean, maybe not the first semester of freshman year, but within the second semester I could see him settling down with some cute girl. *Why am I thinking about this so deeply?* I thought to myself. Finn started to laugh. "Something on your mind?" I think my face gave it away.

"They seem really close," I said. Casey and Finn started to laugh again. Is everything a joke to them or something?

"They are close, but not like before," Finn said. "Rachel broke his heart when she broke up with him. They didn't talk for a good four months. You see, Ethan was moving at the end of junior year. Rachel found out and was devastated. Ethan was willing to do long-distance, since he loved Rachel that much. When he told her he loved her, I think she was shocked. Then out of nowhere, a few weeks later, she dumped him. Ethan was so confused, especially since she didn't give him a reason--Just that it was for the best. Ethan was so pissed at her until around mid-September when she texted him and apologized."

"Since then, their friendship has rebounded," Casey said. I was surprised. Ethan seemed like an outgoing and friendly person; you wouldn't believe he had his heart broken. Then Finn whispered into my ear. "Don't worry too much about Rachel. I think Ethan has his eyes on you."

I looked at Finn and started to burst out laughter. I was laughing so hard tears started to come out of my eyes. I started rolling around on the ground. Finn and Casey laughed at me and then looked up. I stopped rolling around when Ethan said, "What's going on, neighbor?" I stopped laughing and got flustered because Ethan saw me laughing hysterically. I stood up. "Oh, nothing." Ethan grinned and patted my head. "Whatever you say, neighbor." I looked and saw Rachel had her arm around Ethan's arm still. I looked back up at Ethan's face and saw him smiling at me.

"Hey neighbor, I have to show you this one food truck you will definitely like." He grabbed my hand and started running off with me. Rachel was shocked and called out to Ethan, but we kept running away.

After we stopped running, I caught my breath. We were standing in front of a food truck. I looked down and saw Ethan was still holding my hand. He looked at me with a smile on his face. "Look at the truck." Its sign read *Funnel Cakes*. This brought back good memories of when I was little. My family and I always went to amusement parks. Every time we got there, I wanted funnel cake. A smile formed on my face as I thought about the past. I realized I spaced out because Ethan let go of my hand and went to get me a funnel cake. He came back over and smiled. "Here." I took it from him. "Thanks."

"It's no problem. I mean you were eyeing it, so I figured you wanted it. Let's go sit down." We walked over to a vendor who sold blankets for five dollars. Ethan paid for one. We went and sat in the shade. I bit into the funnel cake once I sat down. Ethan sat down and looked up at the sky. "Is the funnel cake good?"

"Yeah, thanks again," I said. I looked over and saw Ethan was smiling at me. "What?"

"Neighbor, you're adorable." He laughed. I was taken back and started to fluster a bit. I had never been called cute before or at least if I had I couldn't remember when. I hit him in the arm a bit.

"Ow, you hurt me," Ethan said. I rolled my eyes and started to laugh. Ethan laughed as well. Then he stole a piece of my funnel cake. I gave him the death stare. Ethan got scared a bit. "Neighbor, don't be mad." I finished the rest of my funnel cake and threw the plate away once I was done. I came back and saw Ethan lying down. I sat down next to him.

"You know something," Ethan said as he was lying down. "Nature is so beautiful. That's what I love about Portland. Nature is everywhere you go. Downtown, it's more urban. But if you go on a trail, you see the beauty of Portland. I think that's why I continue to fall more in love with Portland, day by day." I looked at him. He moved closer to me and put his head on my lap. He slowly fell asleep. I looked at him and messed with his hair. "That feels nice... keep doing that, Aly," Ethan said slowly. I was shocked. *He said my name again.* I decided to keep doing it. I lay down and decided to nap too. Ethan moved in and wrapped his arm around me. I was surprised it didn't trigger a flashback this time. I guess it was because I was comfortable and he made me feel safe in a way. A smile appeared on my face again as I drifted off to sleep.

5:45pm

I woke up. As my body sat up, I rubbed my eyes and saw Ethan, sitting up next to me. He smiled. "Good afternoon, neighbor. Did you sleep well?" I looked at him and yawned. "Yeah." He got up. "Then let's continue on this adventure." He held out his hand. I grabbed it and we walked around. With each other as company.

Thursday: 10:00am

I woke up and rubbed my eyes. Ethan was standing in front of me, with no shirt on. "Ethan?" He looked at me. He had this smirk on his face. "Aly." I was confused. He started to come closer to me. "What's up, Ethan?" He looked at me and put his hand on my cheek. "I forgot something."

"What?" Ethan looked at me. "This"

He kissed me. I closed my eyes. When I opened them, I realized it was all a dream. I touched my lips. *It felt so real though.* I thought. I saw a note next to my bedside table. *Went for a run. Be back soon.* I got out of bed and decided to go eat brunch.

It was noon when I headed back to the room. As I entered the room, I closed the door behind me and headed to my bed. The bathroom door opened and steam came out. I turned around and saw Ethan coming out of the bathroom. He wasn't watching where he was going, since he was drying his hair. He bumped into me and we both started to fall onto the ground. I closed my eyes until I hit the ground. When I opened my eyes, I looked up and saw Ethan fell on top of me. Ethan's pale face turned red when he realized where he fell. "Sorry, neighbor." Then I remembered. *Ethan just came out of the shower.* I looked away and said, "Ethan! Get off of me!" He laughed at me and got up. He smirked. "You know I have pants on. Pervert." I was taken off guard from that comment because I wasn't referring to that. He laughed and moved back over to his side of the room. I got mad at him because he found this funny. Ethan was still giggling. "Neighbor, are you mad at me?" I shrugged my shoulders. I was confused why he called me neighbor instead of my name, so I decided to ask him.

"Ethan, why do you call me neighbor instead of Aly?" I asked as I sat back on my bed.

"Because you're my neighbor, duh," Ethan said with that stupid overjoyed smile on his face. I shrugged my shoulders and opened my laptop.

"So do you have any plans today?" Ethan asked as he put his clothes on.

"Yeah, Casey invited me over to her house." I looked over and Ethan had a smile on his face. "That's awesome."

"Is that cool with you?"

He laughed. "Yeah, I'm hanging out with Finn."

The temptation arose to ask Ethan about the whole Rachel thing since Finn had told me about it, but it didn't feel like my place to ask. He looked at me confused. "Something on your mind, neighbor?" I snapped back to reality. "No." Ethan laughed. "Okay." I realized what time it was and decided to get ready. "When are you leaving?"

"Once I'm dressed, I'm heading over," Ethan said. "Do you want a ride to Casey's house? It's on the way."

"Sure," I said.

"Okay, I'll wait for you to get dressed and we can leave together."

"Okay." I headed to the bathroom to get ready.

2:00pm

Once I got to Casey's house, I knocked on the door. She came to the door and smiled. "Hey, Aly," she said. I smiled back and said, "Hey, Casey."

"Come in." We headed up to her room. Alison was sitting on her bed. "Hey, Aly." I waved to her. Casey sat in her computer chair. I sat on her bed.

"Are we going to the Annual Fall Bash this weekend?" Alison asked.

"What's that?" I asked.

Casey laughed. "I forgot you aren't from here. It's this two-day party thrown in Downtown Portland every fall. The main event is Saturday, but they do this parade and stuff for kids on Friday. They close the main square around six on Saturday and throw a ball in the heart of it. Everyone gets dressed up and goes dancing."

"That sounds fun," I said.

"Yeah, everyone looks forward to it in the fall." Alison got up from the bed. "We should go dress shopping." I laughed. "I'm not going." Casey looked at me. "Why not? Ethan goes every year." She smirked at me. "Plus, he looks good when he is dressed up."

"I don't know if he wants to go." I looked at my phone and saw a text from Ethan. *Do you want to go to the dance together?"* I threw my phone on the ground. Casey picked it up and looked at the message. She smiled hugely. "I'm texting him back yes. Now Aly, let's go shopping."

We went to a local boutique. I looked at my phone and saw it was three forty-five. I sat down waiting for Alison and Casey to come out, so I could give them an opinion on their dresses. Casey picked a dress. "Have you found anything yet, Al?"

"No," I said. I turned around and saw *my dress.*

7:00pm

I ate dinner at Casey's house and she drove me back to the hotel. Once I walked into my room, I saw Ethan lying against his pillows, watching TV. He looked at me with a smile. "Welcome back, neighbor." I put my bag down. "Hey, Ethan."

"How was hanging out with Casey?"

I sat down on my bed. "It was fun."

"That's good, neighbor." He smirked. "Did you go shopping?"

"Maybe."

"Well, I'm excited to go dancing with you Saturday." He started to laugh. "If it's like anything I see through my window, I'm in for a treat." I stuck my tongue out at him.

Saturday: 3:00pm

I went over to Casey's house to get ready. When I got there, Casey and Alison needed to step out really quickly to the drug store for some makeup, so I waited in her room. I was reading a book when I heard a knock on the door. Rachel opened it and came in. When she saw it was me in the room, the smile on her face evaporated. I was confused, but smiled at her. Rachel came in and closed the door behind her. "Hi, Rachel."

Rachel glared. "Save it," she said with a serious tone.

"Is there a problem?"

"I don't appreciate you going with Ethan to the dance."

I raised my eyebrow. Rachel was starting to seem like Katie from back home. "We are just friends."

"I don't care what you guys are, but I did some research on you, Aly Pisano." She turned around. "Nathan, come in." All of a sudden, Nathan was right in front of me. *Nathan. Nathan. Him.* I remembered Nathan had said he was from Portland. He looked at me. "Hey. Good to see you again." I froze up. For the first time since sophomore year, I was scared. He moved closer to me and put his hand on my cheek. I moved my face away. "You look great. Two years does change a person." He started moving his hand down. I softly said, "What do you want?" Rachel snapped her finger and Nathan moved away.

"When I found out my brother and you dated, I was surprised. I was even more surprised when he told me it was a secret fling. I figured this was good blackmail," Rachel said. I didn't look at them. I put my face down because I couldn't face him. It made me feel so sick. "I want you to text Ethan and tell him to go with me. And at the dance, make sure you don't look for him or I might have to let this secret slip out." I started to feel tears in my eyes.

"Okay." I had no choice. It was better to lose Ethan as my dancing partner then have my past secrets shared with him. I looked at Rachel and wondered if she knew what her brother had done. She left the room. Nathan walked over to me one more time. He looked at me and then headed for the door. "Wait," I said. He stopped before walking out the door. "Does she even know what happened?" A tear started to run down my face. Nathan didn't turn around. "No…besides, I told you I'm sorry." He walked out of the room and closed the door behind him.

I fell to the floor and broke down crying. I couldn't believe the guy I once loved and who raped me just stood right in front of me. I cried and cried. I texted Ethan the message Rachel wanted and threw my phone to the other side of the room. I never wanted to see Nathan again. All the feelings I had kept deep down inside of me were pouring out with my tears. I hate him. I hate him so much. He acted like nothing even happened and didn't even tell his sister. If she knew, would she have been more comforting? I lay on the ground and cried. I knew my eyes probably were red from how much I was crying. The door opened and Casey and Alison walked into the room. They saw me and realized I was broken. They helped me up from the floor and sat me on the bed. Casey asked, "What happened, Aly?" I decided to tell them about my past and what happened. When I finished, Casey was shocked.

"It's okay, Aly," Alison said. She wiped away my tears with a tissue. I got up and picked up my phone. Ethan texted me back.

"Guys, I can't go to the dance anymore," I said. "Ethan is going with Rachel. I can't have her tell him about Nathan."

"Don't let that slut stop you from going," Casey said.

"Yeah," Alison said.

"Your past doesn't define you, Aly," Casey said. "We all have done things or had things done to us in the past that we aren't proud of. You learn in life that one incident can't define you unless you want it to. You decide how to handle whatever situation comes your way, but you can't let it hurt or keep you from achieving your full potential." I looked at Casey and smiled a bit. She was right.

"Okay, can you help me get ready for this dance?"

6:00pm

"Voila," Casey said as she put the finishing touch. I looked in the mirror. My dress was a dark, red skater dress that covered my shoulders. It also had a black belt around the stomach area. I put on black tights and boots. Casey pinned up my hair since I braided it for most of the day and she knew a hairstyle. I loved it. My eyes weren't red anymore and I was excited for the dance now. "You look beautiful."

Finn walked in. "You really do. Ethan will be blown away." Alison hit him on the arm. "Hey, I know they aren't going together, but still you're going to kill it."

I smiled. This was the first time in a long time I felt really good about myself. Finn smiled. "Well, if we are all ready, what are we waiting for, Let's go!"

We got our stuff and headed for the dance.

When we got to park square, we had to walk through this path. After we walked in, Finn thought we should head over to the refreshments first. I got water and looked around. I saw Rachel and Ethan walk in together. Rachel's dress was stunning. It was this one strap light blue dress. The strap was on her right shoulder. The chest was beaded with diamonds. It looked kind of like a homecoming dress, but she looked beautiful since her hair was curled. I looked over at Ethan. Casey wasn't kidding when she said Ethan knew how to dress up. I looked at him for a while. Then he turned and looked at me. A smiled appeared on his face. I turned around before Rachel saw us looking at each other. Casey saw me turn around fast. "You saw Ethan and Rachel too?"

"They look great together."

Finn laughed. "Of course they do. That's Rachel for you." The DJ started playing music. The song *Hands to Myself* by Selena Gomez came on. Casey dragged me onto the dance floor. She started to dance. "Come on." I protested. "I can't dance."

"Come on Aly, what do you have to lose?" I started to dance. I let the music go through me. We danced together and then soon Finn and Alison got into it too. I kept dancing and sang with the music.

I want you all to myself
Your metaphorical gin and juice
So come on, give me a taste
Of what it's like to be next to you
Won't let one drop go to waste
Your metaphorical gin and juice

I stopped dancing and sang the chorus with Casey. When the song ended, I bumped into someone. I stopped and turned around. "I'm so sorry." I looked up and saw it was Ethan. I turned around and saw that my friends had gotten lost in the crowd. Ethan smiled. "Hey." I was happy to see him again, so I hugged him. "Hey."

"You look beautiful."

I put a piece of my hair behind my ear. "Thanks." I looked at him. "You don't look bad yourself." I realized what I said. *I'm an idiot.* Ethan laughed and then I laughed as well.

"It's nice to be talking with you. Where's Rachel?"

"No clue. She probably got lost in the crowd with another boy." He laughed. The next song came on. It was my favorite song. Lose it by Oh Wonder. I smiled. "This is my song."

"Let's dance then." We danced together. I spun around and started to lose it. Ethan laughed and continued to dance. I forgot about Ethan being there.

"Move your feet and feel it in the space between… We gotta lose it… Lose it. Lose it. Lose it," I sang along with the music. I closed my eyes and let the music be my guide. I listened to the song and realized the song was right. I needed to lose it and let go of my past. I remembered everything that had happened this week. How I met Casey and how nice she was. The art museum. The street fair and all the good, fatty food I ate. The shopping I did. I started to remember Ethan. **Ethan.** *Ethan.* The guy that brought me on this trip. How much fun the car ride with him was. How he fell on top of me and how embarrassed I got. How he fell asleep in my lap at the fair. How he grabbed me before I fell into the road at the museum and I was in his chest. After all these events, I realized something. Ethan helped me. In a way, this trip was meant for him to come back and see his friends and I was just tagging along, but he helped me bring back this person I used to really love. I felt like he opened me up to so many things. To take risks. To go headfirst into situations. He helped me bring back a part of myself I thought was gone. He brought back my hope. I realized Ethan helped me feel safe. He helped me learn how to let go and lose it. As I looked at him, I felt this knot in my stomach. Then I realized something. Ethan brought back the person I lost when I was raped and told I wasn't loved by the one person I loved the most. I held my hand out. Ethan grabbed it, brought me in, and spun me out. I let go and spun. Then spun back to Ethan. He held my back and brought me into him. We looked at each other. The song started to slow down. Ethan moved his hand to my cheek. He started to rub it. I closed my eyes and listened to the music. We danced in each others arms. The song started to come to the ending verse.

Move your feet and feel it in the space between
You gotta give yourself a moment, let your body be

We gotta lose it
We gotta lose it

I opened my eyes and realized Ethan was looking at me. I saw Ethan's face move closer.

And we kissed.

EIGHT

8:00pm

We stopped kissing. My heart felt like it had stopped and my mind was racing. Ethan just kissed me. *Ethan. Kissed. Me.* I felt like everything I had believed in for so long was falling apart. I kissed a boy. This boy was Ethan. I didn't like him like that. We had a great friendship and I loved how we clicked. How he helped me open this closed door I had sealed for so long. How he convinced me to open up. Let go and lose it. I stood there. Ethan looked at me. He scratched the back of his head. "Sorry." I was still shocked, so I said, "U-ummm, it's okay." Rachel came out of nowhere and stood next to Ethan. When she saw me in front of him, she looked at him and kissed him right in front of me. I felt that knot still in my stomach. I know what my feelings were for Ethan, because all I could think about was everything we did together this past week. I couldn't think about this because Ethan was with Rachel. So I did what I was good at: I turned around and ran. I heard Ethan call out my name, but I just kept running. I passed by Casey, Finn, and Alison as I ran out of the park. I took off my shoes and kept running back to the hotel.

I made it back to the hotel and went up to our room. I looked at my phone and saw the missed calls from my friends. *I'm sorry.* I turned off my phone. I didn't know what I would say, so I decided to close them out. I took off my dress and threw it into my luggage. I went to the bathroom and looked at myself. A tear started running down my face. I washed my face and wiped it dry with a hand towel. My hair looked a mess, so the braid came out. I turned off the bathroom light and headed back into the room. I knew what I had to do. I had to leave. I felt that knot returning to my stomach again. I understood what this feeling was and what it meant. It was the same thing with the kiss I shared with Ethan. I touched my lips and remembered. It felt like it lasted for so long, but at the same time it was taken away just like that. I mean, I have lived the past three years not believing in "relationships" and the one person I had a connection with goes and kisses me. The last thing I wanted to do is talk about our "future". I decided to pack my stuff and take a bus home. Another tear ran down my face. I looked at the clock on the wall. It was five minutes after nine. I heard a knock on the door. I knew who it was. Ethan.

"Aly?" He called out. I didn't say anything. He put the key card in and opened the door. He walked in and saw me standing there. He walked over with this serious expression on his face. He hugged me tightly. He looked at me and said with a serious tone," What the hell was that, Aly?" Why did you run away?" I couldn't look at him, so I looked at the ground. "I-I-I don't know."

"That was so reckless. Everyone was worried about you. I was really worried. Especially when you didn't answer my calls.

"I turned my phone off." I started to feel tears come down my face.

He looked at me with a softer face expression. "What's wrong?" He put a hand on my cheek. "Why are you crying?"

I softly said, "I'm fine." I made eye contact with him this time. I tried to made the tears stop. "I'm sorry if I scared you."

Ethan had a serious tone as he said, "Why are you lying, Aly?" He looked at me. It felt like he was looking more at my heart then he was at me. "I'm sorry if the kiss scared you. Aly, I have been wanting to kiss you for awhile. Because…because… I am in love with you, Aly Pisano. I want to kiss you again. But I won't if you don't want me to. Tell me right now." He started to move closer to me and kissed me. I didn't stop him because I knew this would be our last kiss together. I wanted to cherish it. The kiss grew deeper as I lay down on my bed. When Ethan kissed my neck, a flashback came back to me and I shouted. Ethan stopped kissing me. I pushed him away. He stood up, confused. "What's wrong?"

"I-I-I am really thirsty," I said. "Can you get me some ice for my water?"

He smiled. "Sure." He walked out of the room to go get my ice. I realized this was my only chance. I grabbed my stuff and headed for the elevator. Once I got in, I pushed the lobby button. Ethan turned a corner and dropped the ice. He started to run for the elevator.

"Aly, don't leave!" He called out.

I couldn't stay. This was the only thing I knew how to do when problems came up in my life. Run away from it. That's what I did went my parents got a divorce. I ran away to downtown Seattle. That's where I met Nathan. Then when Nathan broke my heart, I ran away from the problem by closing people out. Running away from a situation is what I was kind of good at. Once I reached the lobby, I asked a lady at the front desk when the next shuttle was leaving. She told me at nine forty-five. I looked at my phone and saw it was nine forty-three, so I headed for the bus stop. Once I was outside, I saw the bus coming. Ethan came out of the door and said, "Aly… don't leave."

I knew I could turn around and run right into his arms. I could kiss him and tell him "Okay, I won't leave. We can figure out everything." Tell him I was in love with him. Then we could be happy and in love, but then I remembered something. My life isn't a romantic movie where I get the boy or the love I deserve because I don't believe in "true love" or "happy endings".

Ethan softly said, "Do you even love me back? I feel like you do, so if I'm right don't leave. But if I'm not, I'll know your answer."

That knot feeling was still in my stomach. I knew I couldn't stay. I couldn't let this knot control me or break someone's heart.

"Well then you know my answer."

The shuttle stopped in front of me and I got on. The door closed behind me. It felt like the doors on our friendship had closed as well. I sat at a window seat. I didn't look at the hotel as we passed by it. The minute we turned the corner, I knew.

The best friendship that had came into my life was gone.

Just like the hope and happiness Ethan brought back this week into my life was gone as well.

NINE

November- Three week since the trip

Monday: 8:45am

I looked at the ground and saw a wine bottle. *Completely Empty.* I sat up from my bed, as the hangover started creeping over me. I smelled myself and decided a shower was a must today. As the water warmed up, the past three weeks came back to me. I got home from Portland and my mom was shocked to see me. I told her I was sick and wanted to come home early, but let Ethan stay behind. I couldn't tell her the truth obviously. I thought Ethan would act differently to me on Monday, but to my surprise he was completely indifferent to me. If I spoke to him, he would smile and talk back to me. One thing that was different was he never looked at me like he used to. I brushed my teeth, knowing that couldn't get the scent of alcohol off of my mouth, so a piece of gum it was. After my shower, I threw on joggers, a V- neck t-shirt and black Converse. It was cold in Washington today, so my winter coat was a must. I made my way downstairs with my stuff in my hand. My mom left early for work today, so I grabbed an apple and headed out the door. Ethan was walking over to his car too. I waved at him. Ethan looked at me and waved back before getting into his car and driving off. I threw my stuff in the passenger seat once I got into my car. Once I put the key into the ignition, I drove off to school.

10:50am

While in Math class, my mind couldn't focus. Too much was happening inside of it. The last place I wanted to be was school. Preston looked over at me. He tapped my shoulder to get my attention. I looked at him. He whispered, "You smell like you had a good time last night."

"Is it that strong?" I was shocked he could smell the wine on me still.

"I think it's only because I'm sitting next to you. I can smell it, but anyone in the front probably couldn't smell it.

I sighed. "Oh well." He looked at me with this concerned face.

"I will be okay, Preston."

"Okay, if you say so." I smiled at him. "Thanks." I started to listen to the lesson again. I realized Preston actually can be a good person.

2:45pm

Sam and I headed to our cars. Sam was talking about something, but I was kind of out of it until I ran into Ethan by my car. I looked at him and he looked back at me.

"Sorry."

Ethan smiled. "It's cool. See you around." He got into his car and drove off.

Sam was confused. "What was going on between you two?"

"I can't talk about this right now." Sam got closer to me. She gave me a serious look. "Have you been drinking again, Aly?"

"I did. Last night."

Sam gave me this serious look. "What's going on, Aly?"

"I'm not really sure myself. Bye Sam." I got in my car and headed home. Once I got home, I did the same routine I had done for the past three weeks. Dropped my bag on the floor of my room. Fall into my bed and cry. Then eventually fall asleep. Today was different because Mason was waiting for me in my room.

"Hey," I said as I sat on my bed.

"What's going on with you, Aly," Mason asked me with a serious tone. I had my hands on my lap, so Mason put his hand on top of mine. I started to feel tears come out of my eyes. I decided to tell Mason what happened in Portland. The true story.

December

Friday before Christmas break: Lunch

After I explained everything with Mason, I stopped drinking on the weekends alone in my room. I ate my lunch and enjoyed my friends company.

"What is everyone doing for Christmas?" Sam asked the table. "Aly, you go first."

"I'm going to Colorado with my mom and siblings," I said. "John is going to propose to my mom and we are kind of in on it."

"That's so cute," Sam said.

"That's awesome," Mason said.

I smiled because I was pretty happy that my mom found an amazing guy like John.

"That's really cool, Aly," Ethan said. The whole table was shocked.

"Ethan, you said her name," Jake said.

Ethan laughed. "Did I?"

"Yeah...you never call her by her first name," Sam said.

Ethan laughed again. "Well, I guess things change."

Sam laughed. "Yeah, I guess so."

I knew things had changed...a lot.

Christmas Break: Colorado

Monday: 2:30pm

My mom, Nick, Hollie, and I finally landed in Colorado. John was waiting for us. He had a sign with our last names on it. My mom laughed at him. "You're a big goof."

"Well at least I'm your goof," John said. My mom smiled and kissed him.

"Too much PDA," Nick said. He put a finger in his mouth and acted like he was throwing up. I hit him in the arm, so he would shut up. John laughed and led us to his car. We headed to the cabin we were staying at. When we got there, I headed to my room. I started to unpack my stuff and changed into warmer clothes. Once I finished, I headed downstairs and saw the Christmas tree. I smiled at how big it was and headed back up to my room. My brother came in with John's PS4. John brought it with him to the cabin. I lay down on the bed.

"What's up, Al-man," Nick said as he set up the PS4.

I smiled. "It's been awhile since I have heard that name."

"Yeah, ha-ha."

As we played Uncharted, we caught up. Nick told me how college was going for him. He explained how next summer he is probably going to intern somewhere.

"Have you heard back from any schools?"

"Yeah, Iowa, UW, Pace and UP. I applied to University of Southern California back in September and I got an email on Saturday that I got in. So I got into all the schools I applied too!"

"Congrats, little sis." He hugged me and had this huge smile on his face.

"Thanks, I'm not sure which one I am going to go to yet."

"Do you have a school you are going more towards?"

"Probably, Iowa and USC."

Nick smiled. "Well, don't stress too much about it. It will all work out in the end."

"Yeah, that's true." I toured Iowa last spring and fell in love with the campus. But in the summer we toured USC on our way back from Europe. The campus was beautiful. The idea of getting far away from Seattle was a nice idea as well. Plus, it wasn't always raining in the SoCal. I honestly could see myself going either place. At USC, I would have to pay private tuition, which wasn't a big issue for me, but I wasn't fully sure yet if I wanted to go there or not. Hollie came into my room. "Can I join you guys?"

Nick rolled his eyes as he played. "Finee." Hollie never enjoyed video games like Nick and I did. This was because most of the time she was a real girly girl. Hollie joined us and tried to play as Drake. She sucked, but I enjoyed this. I loved how close my siblings and I were because it made life a little brighter when we were all together. When our parents got a divorce, they kind of distanced themselves from my parents and me as well. It kind of sucked, but after that year they started to reach out more. Then all of a sudden, my big mouth ruined it.

"Oh my god, I love you Ethan."

My eyes got big and I realized what I just said. Of course, I would ruin this nice moment with my family. That knot in my stomach started to tighten. I hoped my siblings didn't hear what I said. Nick paused the game and asked, "Who's Ethan?"

I sighed and knew I had to explain everything, so I did. My siblings listened to everything I told them and at the end I asked them, "What should I do?"

Nick was shocked. Hollie was so happy for me. So happy that she hugged me. "My baby sister is in love, this is great."

"This is not okay," Nick said.

"Don't worry about Nick," Hollie said. "Nick's protective brother powers are kicking in." Nick rolled his eyes and decided to go and get something to eat.

"What should I do, Hollie?" I asked. Hollie looked at me and held my hand.

"Aly," She said with a serious tone. "You can't control who you fall in love with, but you do control how you will go about these feeling." She got up. "You will figure it out." She smiled and left my room. I lay back on my bed and looked up at the ceiling. Ethan came to my mind. Wondering what he was doing back in Washington. The knot in my stomach wasn't as tight as it was before. I wanted to talk with him, but I knew the last person he would want to hear from was me. I started to miss that stupid gleeful smile. I picked up my pillow and put it in my face.

I hoped that next semester would be a lot better than this one.

TEN

New Year: January

Monday: 8:45am

I woke up and realized it was the first day back to school in the new year. While rubbing my eyes and yawing, I walked over to my mirror, and decided to wear a black dress with tights and booties, since it was the first day back. My hair was natural today. I grabbed my stuff and went downstairs to toast a waffle and cut some fruit.

"Good morning," My mom said as she came into the kitchen.

"Morning," I said as I put my food on my plate, grab a bottle of OJ out of the fridge, and sat down at the countertop.

"Your outfit is very nice." She smiled at me.

I smiled after I took a sip of my juice. "Thanks." She started to prepare something for herself as I kept eating. When done, I cleaned up my spot and headed for the door.

"Have a great day back to school!" She blew me a kiss and had this huge smile on her face.

"Thanks, mom. Love you!" She closed the door behind me as I headed to my car. Ethan was leaving his house too. I hurried to my car because I didn't want to see him this morning. Once in, I backed out and headed off to school.

School: 9:00am

I headed to Creative Writing class. Since figuring out my feelings for Ethan over break, I thought I was ready to face them head on. *I mean I just liked him, how bad could it be to confess that to him?* I thought. Ethan walked into the class with this huge smile on his face. The same gleeful smile I hated. As my eyes looked at him, this smile was forming on my face. I covered my mouth with my hands and realized how wrong I was. I put my head down on my desk. *Ughhhhh I hate this.* I thought. Ethan made it over to our table and patted the top of my head. "Your hair is so big." I looked at him and nodded. "Anyway, good morning, Aly. How was your Christmas break?" I looked at him and got captivated by his hazel eyes like always. His eyes were probably his best feature. Everything about him was pretty hot, but his eyes were different. They looked safe, like if you were with him you would be okay.

"It was good. Colorado was cold and I'm happy to be back in Washington."

"Well that's good." I laughed. "Yeah. What did you do over the holiday?"

"My family from California came up to see us. It was really fun being with that part of my family."

"I'm sure it was if they are anything like you." I laughed. He hit my shoulder lightly. "What does that mean, neighbor?"

"Ohhh nothing." Mr. Smith came into the room and class began. He told the class we were going to begin our Poetry unit. We would have to write a poem expressing something and would be presenting our own poems on Thursday. I hated poetry. It's not because it's hard to understand the meaning or something. Its because of Nathan. I used to love poetry, but not anymore. It's actually the reason I probably fell for him. *What an idiot I am.* I realized Mr. Smith wasn't talking anymore. I looked over and saw Ethan wasn't next to me anymore. I looked around and saw Katie and him talking. That weird knot in my stomach came back, so my headphones went in to shut everyone out. After thirty minutes passed, the bell rang and I rushed the hell out of that class.

I didn't take my headphones out until I walked into English. Preston made a comment to me. Paying no attention to the comment, I walked to my desk and sat down. My mind ponded on why Ethan was talking with Katie. It didn't make sense to me. Yes, Ethan is a friendly guy, but never did he once talk to her in class last semester. Then again last semester we weren't as distant to each. I sighed and realized life honestly does suck. Cara waved her hand in my face.

"You daydream too much," Cara said with a laugh.

I laughed. "Yeah, it's a bad habit."

Mrs. Sheppard told us we would be doing this *Pride and Prejudice* project with assigned partners. She told us it would be due two Mondays from now. After she finished explaining to us and answering questions, she told us who our partners were. Cara got partnered with Conner. We looked over at him and he started high fiving his buddies. Cara rolled her eyes and put her finger in her mouth like she was going to throw up. I waited to hear who my partner was. I didn't have any problem working with anyone really in the class except... Preston. When Mrs. Sheppard finally got to my name, she said Preston. I realized I was stuck with this douche for the next two weeks. *FML.* After telling us our partners, she gave us the rest of class to come up with a plan for our projects.

"Aly, come over here," Preston called out. "I don't want to move over there." I got up and sat next to him. We were supposed to read *Pride and Prejudice* over the break. I had read it before we were assigned, so I knew what scene we could do.

"Did you read the book?" I asked Preston. I knew Preston never read the books because in Math he would talk with the person next to us about how he probably failed that test or something.

"Yeah, I did," Preston said. "I read it while going to a soccer tournament in the car and whenever I had a chance over the break."

I was shocked. "Well since we have to recreate a scene for our project, do you just want to come over to my house and we figure out everything later this week? My siblings will probably be home, but they won't bother us."

I looked at him when he said that. Preston and I weren't that close. The only time we ever really talked was in Math when he didn't understand something. "Will your parents be okay with that?"

"Well, they won't be home until late, so it's probably fine. Plus, we will be working on a project, so why would they worry about that? I mean, we aren't making out with each other on the side." He started surfing his phone. I realized there was no getting out of this invitation.

"Does Wednesday work for you?"

"Yeah, that's okay. This is my cell phone number and address." He took my phone and put his contact information in it. I walked back over to my desk. The bell rang and I left.

Wednesday: 3:45pm

After checking the time, I changed into leggings and a big t-shirt. Then grabbed my stuff and headed to Preston's house. I texted him once I was in the car that I was heading over. He texted: *okay, see you soon* ☺. I backed out and headed over to Preston's house. Once there and parked, I made my way to his front door. Waiting for someone to open the door, my eyes looked around. Then I heard someone say," Hello, can I help you?" A fourteen-year-old boy stood in front of me. I smiled and said, "Hi, I'm Aly. Is Preston home?"

The kid smiled. "Yeah, he is home. Are you his girlfriend? You're really pretty, so you must be."

I laughed because ew. "No, we have a project we are working on together."

"Oh, okay. My name is Easton. Nice to meet you, Aly. You can come in." I walked in and he closed the door. This kid was really adorable. Preston and Easton looked a lot alike, but Easton was cuter obviously.

"You're so adorable." Easton got shy. "Awe, thanks." He looked up at the top of the stairs and Preston was standing there.

"Well speak of the devil, you're here," Preston said with a smirk. I rolled my eyes. "You can come upstairs and leave Easton alone."

"Preston, be nice to Aly," Easton said. "I mean you never have girls over so this one must be special." Preston rolled his eyes. "Aly come upstairs." He started to walk away.

"Bye Easton." I walked upstairs and followed him. We went into his room. I was surprised by what I saw. His room was nice. He had a full-size bed with dark blue sheets and a comforter. He had a few soccer trophies from little league soccer all the way up until now. He also had a picture of Cristiano Ronaldo hung up on his wall. It was interesting. He also had a TV up against his wall and a couch in between his bed and the TV. He sat down on his couch. "You can sit down next to me," Preston said without looking at me. "I won't bite." He started to play Assassin's Creed again.

"Okay, so I had a few ideas on how we could film it," I said. "We could film against a wall and take turns acting out the scene we decide to do."

"Yeah."

"Or if you want we could be talking to one and other but from different angles."

"Yeah."

"I like that way better because then we can film all of one person's scene while one person is manning the camera."

"Cool." I looked over to Preston. He wasn't paying attention to anything I was saying because he was so focused on Assassin's Creed.

"Oh my god, Preston," I said in an angry tone. "If all you're going to do is play video games while we are working on this project, I don't think this will work out." I got up and headed to the door. As I walked out, I bumped into Alex, Preston's other brother. Alex looked at me with his annoyed face. "Who are you?"

"I'm so sorry," I said. "I'm Aly Pisano. I'm working on a project with Preston."

"Are you guys dating?"

I laughed. "Nope. Just partners for this assignment."

Alex looked at me and rolled his eyes. "Next time, watch where you're going." He walked away and went downstairs. I stood there confused about what I did to him. Preston touched my shoulder. He grabbed my hand and pulled me back into his room.

"Sorry about Alex, he's kind of a douche." I looked and saw he had turned off the TV. "Look, I'm sorry I wasn't listening, but I do want a good grade on this project, so I'll listen to what you say now." He smiled and looked genuinely sorry. I smiled.

"Okay, let's get to work."

A week later

Wednesday: 4:00pm

We started filming last weekend, but didn't finish. Preston came to pick me up, so we would finish it all that afternoon. He texted me.

I'm here. I walked out of my door and saw his Honda CR-V next to my curb. I opened the passenger door. "Hey." I smiled as I buckled up. "Hello." He smiled back. He started his car again and we drove off. We both were hungry, so we decided to get pizza before heading to his house. "I'll pay for it," Preston said.

"Okay," I said. "How much do I owe you?"

He laughed. "Don't worry about it. It's on me."

I smiled. "Thanks, Preston." We got the pizza and headed back to his house.

By the time we reached Preston's house, it was five. Once we walked into the house, we went to the kitchen. Preston got plates for the two of us. He handed one to me.

"Thanks," I said. I opened the pizza box and got two slices of cheese pizza.

Preston went over to his fridge. "What do you want to drink?"

"Water, please." He got me a glass of water and put it in front of me. Then got two slices of pizza. We sat at the countertop and ate our pizza.

"This pizza is so good," I said.

"Agreed," Preston said with a smile. "This is nice."

"What?"

"This. It's nice how we are just hanging out together eating pizza and chilling. We aren't using illegal drugs or partaking in illegal actions to have fun. I don't know, it's just nice." I was confused where this was coming from, so I decided to ask him a question.

"I got a question for you."

"What's up?"

"Why do you act differently when we're alone? You act one way with your friends and then another when it's just you and I? I'm confused."

He sighed. "I'll explain. I have this image I have to keep up. Sometimes I hate it because I would rather be eating pizza and hanging out with people like you, Aly. For me, that's not the case. Don't get me wrong, I love my friends and they are awesome, but I wished we could chill more at home then go to parties, get drunk, and act like complete assholes. The thing is I don't remember how I was at parties until a few days later, which is the wrong part about the whole thing."

I felt badly for him. "Is it becoming a problem?"

Preston laughed. "No. I haven't gone out since soccer is starting up soon and I want to be in the best condition possible." I laughed. "Yeah, that's true. You're not that bad, Preston Chase." He smiled at me. "Neither are you, Aly Pisano." He finished his water and looked over at me. "What's going on with that Ethan guy?"

I was shocked a bit from him saying Ethan's name. I mean I had feelings for him, but I couldn't tell Preston that. "It's a very complicated situation." He laughed. "Those are the worst. I hope you guys figure it out because it looked like you guys had a great friendship. Something like that is life changing and shouldn't just end so quickly."

I laughed. "You're right." We cleaned up and headed back up to Preston's room.

It was seven when we finished filming, so Preston decided we should just chill and play video games. I looked at him and smiled. "Thanks for getting the project done." He looked over at me with this surprised look. He smiled. "No problem." A few minutes passed and

Preston's mom, Traci, walked into the room. "Preston...you didn't—oh that's right you said you were having a friend come over. You must be Aly? Preston you didn't tell me she was very pretty."

"Thank you," I said with a smile.

"Well, Preston, dinner is ready," Traci said. "Aly, would you like to join us?"

I knew my mom wouldn't mind if I stayed a little longer. "Sure, Why not?" I smiled. Traci smiled and walked back downstairs.

"You didn't have to stay," Preston said softly.

"It's no big deal," I said. "Your mom seems really nice."

He started to get up from the couch. "Yeah, she's a pretty cool mom, but my dad and brothers are weird."

I laughed. "Easton was a sweetheart. I mean Alex kind of seemed mean." He laughed. "Alex is kind of like that if he doesn't know you that well, but once you become friends with him he's actually really nice."

"Whatever you say. Let's head to dinner." I smiled at him. He smiled back and we headed downstairs.

Aly's house: 9:00pm

Preston took me home after dinner. It was pretty interesting eating dinner with the Chase family. His mom asked me to come over again. Once we arrived at my house, Preston parked on the curb. We got out and walked to my porch. We stood there. He wasn't going to say anything, so I said. "Thanks for the ride. You didn't have to walk me to the door, you know that right?"

"Ha-ha, yeah, but it's fine. Today was fun. I enjoyed hanging out with you again."

I laughed. "Yeah, it was interesting." He smiled at me. "Yes it was. Okay, I'm going to get going. Bye, Aly." I waved bye to him once he got into his car. A smile appeared on my face. He waved back with a smile on his face and drove off. I looked over to Ethan's house and saw him taking out the trash. We looked at each other. I waved at him. He just smiled and walked back into his house. I was confused why he just smiled at me and didn't wave back. I walked into my house, confused, and wondering what the hell was going on.

March

Saturday: 6:30pm

Mason told us at lunch that Ryder was throwing a house party since the soccer season was going well and the team wanted to celebrate. I decided to go and went over to Sam's house to get ready.

"I'm so excited to go to this party with you Al," Sam said.

I surfed on my phone while Sam got ready. "It's going to be fun. Plus, Preston and Ethan will be there." I looked straight at Sam. "What does that mean?" Sam smirked. "Nothing." When Sam was ready, we headed for the party.

We arrived at Ryder's house. When you enter the door, there were people everywhere. From the living room to the kitchen, people talking, drinking, and even people making out with each other.

"Wow." I was shocked because there were so many people around.

"Aly!" Ryder said as he came over. "I'm glad you guys came. Drinks are over there and food is in the kitchen. Have fun and enjoy your time." He walked away to greet other people. Sam decided to head over for the fruit punch.

"Be careful, because it's probably been spiked," I said to her as she ran over.

"Yeah... I will," Sam said. I started to look around the room to see if I knew anyone. I saw a few people from my classes. Then saw Preston with all the other soccer players. He drank a bit from his cup. I looked on the other side and saw Ethan. He was standing over with Brandon and Mason. They were talking about something funny because this huge smile appeared on his face. For some reason, a smile appeared on my face. Ethan looked over in my direction. We made eye contact. I turned around and decided to get some fruit punch. I poured myself a cup and took a sip. The drink was strong, but very sweet so you won't know there was alcohol in it unless you were an experienced drinker and could tell the different between drinks. I downed the whole cup. Sam came back over to me and we headed over to Mason. We hung out with him and a few of his friends. I refilled my cup a few times. When I went to fill it up one more time, Preston came over to me.

"Hey," He said.

"Hey," I said as I poured more fruit punch.

"Can we go talk somewhere away from your friends?" He whispered in my ear. Ethan was in the corner of my vision. When he saw me, I whispered in Preston's ear too. "Sure." We walked over to the other side of the house, where not a lot of people were.

I turned around and looked at Preston.

"You know something? You're pretty hot." The smell of his breath made me realize he was wasted. I started to remember how Preston said he was different when he was drunk. I realized this was a bad idea, so I said, "Thanks, Preston...you seem a bit drunk."

He smirked. "Yeahh, but I still see how beautiful you are." He grabbed my hand with a force and pulled me closer to him. I knew where this was going.

"Preston... what are you doing?" I tried to push him away, but he wouldn't back off. He started to move his hands down my chest. He started to unbutton my shirt. "Aly...we have gotten so close. Why don't we get closer?" A flashback of Nathan came back to me and I started to freak out. "Preston, stop please!" I yelled. As he kept touching me, it started to trigger flashbacks. Mason and Ethan came over to the side we were on. Mason pulled me into his arms when he realized what was going on. "Aly, are you okay?" He had this serious tone in his voice. I started to cry. I couldn't help it: I had finally cracked and it was spilling out.

"What did you do to her?" Ethan asked.

Preston smirked. "Back off, you lost your chance with her loser." Mason moved over to Preston and punched him right in the cheek. Preston fell to the ground. "Take Aly home for me please, she needs to get out of here."

Ethan held out his hand. "Let's go."

"Make sure Sam gets home safely!" I looked at Ethan's eyes and realized I was going to be safe with him. I took his hand. We interlocked our fingers with one another.

We ran out of Ryder's house hand in hand.

ELEVEN

Ethan's house: 11:00pm

We arrived in Ethan's driveway. I had curled up in the passenger seat while Ethan was driving. We didn't speak to one another. He got out of the car and opened my door. He held out his hand. I took it and got out of the car. I looked at the ground as I rubbed my wrist. The grip of Preston's hand still felt like it was there. I remained quiet. Ethan broke the silence.

"Will you be okay being at home tonight?" Ethan asked. I looked at him. I remembered my mom wasn't going to be home tonight, so I would be all alone.

"C-could I stay with you tonight? I really don't want to be alone right now. Not in this state." Ethan was shocked. He rubbed the back of his head. "Sure, I guess. I'll be alone too." We headed over to his house. Ethan unlocked his front door and we went into the house. We went into the kitchen and he made me something to eat. "You must be hungry." I sat at the countertop and didn't say anything back. Ethan made me some pancakes. He got me some water to drink with it. He put the plate and the water in front of me. "Eat." He sat down next to me while I was eating. I ate the food and drank the water.

"Are you okay now?"

I softly said, "Yeah... thanks again." Ethan smiled at me. "It's no problem." I finished the food and Ethan cleaned it up for me.

"Where's your bathroom?"

"Upstairs, to your right." I headed upstairs and went to the bathroom. I threw up into the toilet. *There goes good food.* When I finished, I washed my face. I looked at myself in the mirror and then at my shirt and saw how it was still unbuttoned. I closed my eyes and sighed while leaving the bathroom and headed to Ethan's room. I walked in and Ethan was sitting in his chair. He turned around and looked at me. He smiled. "Do you want to wear something else?" I nodded my head. He gave me one of his big shirts and unused boxers I could wear. I went into his bathroom and changed. When I came out, Ethan had a shirt and sweatpants on. "You can sleep in the bed. I'll probably sleep on the floor or my couch." I sat on the bed and looked at my phone. Mason texted me. *Hey, are you okay?* I texted back. *Yeah, I'm okay now.*

Go to sleep. We can talk more tomorrow.

Good night, Mason. Thank you.

I put my phone on the bed side table. Ethan moved his computer chair closer to me. He looked at me. "Aly... you don't have to, but can we talk about what happened?" I was taken back by his question. I looked at his eyes again and realized he was really concerned with how I was and what happened. Those hazel eyes made me feel so safe, so I decided to tell him about what happened. The true story.

"My parents got divorced the summer before my sophomore year," I said in a serious tone. "It affected me a lot because I was the only one left in the house since my brother and sister were both away at college. My birthday was in the Fall, so I just had to make it to then. When I finally turned sixteen and got my license, I went up to downtown Seattle to get away from my parents. I told them I was going to see my sister, but really I was just running away from my problems at home even if it was for a few hours. A friend of mine lived up in Seattle, so one Friday night she took me to a band performance. We were in the front row. The music was good and I could totally relate to the lyrics. I looked up at the lead singer. We looked at each other and then he looked away. I got flustered and danced around to the music. Once the performance ended, my friend wanted to introduce me to some of her friends there. Then the lead singer came out and introduced himself to us. We looked at each other. He told me his name was Nathan and I told him my name. We talked for a little bit. He told me he went to Seattle U and was 18 years old. We kept getting to know each other until I realized it was getting late and I needed to get some rest. Nathan asked me to come back to their performance next week, and I told him, I'll try my best. After that night, I went up to the city every other weekend. This was to see Nathan. Over a month, we started to get closer to one another. He gave me his number at the end of a show. I smiled and was filled up with so much happiness. It was nice. It was nice not feeling sad anymore because I felt happy, especially when I was talking with Nathan. We started hanging out around town. He read me poems and song ideas, and I realized I liked this guy. I wasn't sure if he felt the same way, too. One night, when I went to a show and it ended, I went outside to see if he would come looking for me. He came out. I was up against a wall. He came closer to me. I flirted with him."

"Want to know something?" I said.

"What?" Nathan asked.

"I really want to kiss you."

"Oh.' He looked at me and kissed me. I kissed him back and that started our secret affair for over six months. Every weekend I went up; I would just stay at his place. It was always a fun time being with him. He would make breakfast, play silly games, and we would work on our writing. It was nice to finally be happy. The darkness that had been casted over me a few months ago felt gone. That was until March. When I realized I was in love with him. I mean it was going to happen eventually. He was this happiness in my shitty life. One weekend, I felt like he loved me back. I went over to his place and we started making out. Things were starting to get a little out of hand. "Nathan, I want to lose my virginity when I know I'm in love with the person I'm having sex with and they love me back." He smiled back. "Okay, Aly whatever makes you happy." It seemed like nothing could go wrong. I was wrong because life for me wasn't this marvelous and it was bound to go to shit eventually."

I took a sip of my water and realized what I was about to tell Ethan. I was going to tell him about that night. The night my life was changed forever.

"It all changed the following weekend. My mom was going out of town, so I invited Nathan over around six. He didn't show up until eight. When I opened the door, I realized he took an Uber because his car wasn't in my driveway. I smelt the whiskey on him, so I figured he was little drunk. "Do you want water?" He nodded his head. We went to my kitchen. I got us two glasses and put water in them. I ran to the bathroom really quick. I realized I loved him and wanted to tell him at the perfect time that night. It seemed like he loved me as well. I came back to the kitchen and we headed up stairs. We went to my room and watched TV on the edge of my bed. I took a sip of my water and put it on my bedside table. A few minutes passed and I felt dizzy and everything was starting to get blurry. Nathan started to kiss my neck.

"I don't feel good," I said.

"I can help you feel good," Nathan said. He started to get blurry as well.

"Nathan, please stop." He didn't stop. He pushed me down on the bed.

"Nathan! Stop! Stop! Stop! Why would you do this if you love me like I love you?" I was shocked it came out like that. He stopped and looked at me. He started to laugh.

"Silly girl, I could never love you. I just want your ass." I felt him started to unbutton my shirt as everything around me went black."

I started to feel tears come down my eyes. *Keep going Aly, you got this!*

"I woke up the next morning and saw I was wearing a big t-shirt. I was confused because I didn't remember changing out of my clothes. I rubbed my eyes and went into the bathroom. I looked at the trash can and saw a used condom wrapper. I started to freak out because I didn't remember anything from last night. I went back into my room and saw Nathan with his head down. I looked at him.

"What...happened...last night?" He looked at me with these eyes of regret. He got up and walked over to me. "Aly?" I showed him the used condom wrapper.

"...you were drunk last night...how?" I felt tears running down my face.

"Aly...I'm really sorry. I-I-I" I realized what happened. I started to cry. "I-I-I t-told you I was a virgin...and it meant a lot to me to keep it." He touched my cheek. "Aly...please I'm sorry. You can't tell anyone what happened. It was an accident. A drunk mistake."

"Get out of my house."

"Aly..."

"GET THE HELL OUT OF MY HOUSE." Nathan grabbed his stuff and left. I sat there and realized what happened to me. Raped by the person I loved and cared about the most. The one person who brought me some kind of joy in my shitty life. I felt like my heart had just broken into so many piece and burned into ashes. I cried and cried and cried for the rest of the day."

Once I finished talking, I realized I was crying. Ethan looked at me and hugged me tightly. "I'm so sorry Aly. I can't believe you went through that. It's not your fault."

"I know," I said still crying. "Ethan, I'm really sorry I left you back in Portland. If I stayed, Rachel would have told you about Nathan. I wasn't ready for you to know about him. I mean I did see him again the day of the bash."

"What?"

I laughed and then started to cry again. Ethan wiped away my tears. He looked at me. "Aly, its okay. You're safe." I looked back at him.

"Thanks for listening."

"No problem," Ethan said. "But I want to tell you my story. My parents got a divorce when I was twelve. At first, it didn't seem as that big of a deal. That was until we settled in Portland and I went to middle school. I started to feel depressed and lonely since my older siblings were gone as well. I didn't want my younger sister to find out what was happening, so I faked my happiness. I went to school and acted like everything was okay. That was until I met Rachel. Rachel changed my life forever. We became best friends. She became a big part of my happiness. When Rachel and I started dating, we just hung out more alone together, then in a group. Rachel realized I was unhappy with life. She couldn't understand what it felt like to have to go through divorce, but she realized I must have been close with my mom in some way since every time I came over I hung out with her mom from time to time. She realized not seeing her all the time was hurting me.

"Ethan, you can't let this incident define how you feel. You deserve to be happy. Yeah, it sucks that you can't see your mom, but it's okay. She would want you to be happy. She wouldn't want her decision to make you feel sad or like its your fault because its not," Rachel said to me.

"After that day, I changed my life. I stopped focusing on the divorce and lived my life for me. I'm glad I listened to Rachel back then because I love who I am today."

He looked at me and held my hand. "Aly... you can't hold this inside of you any longer. You need to tell your parents or someone even if it was two years ago. This incident will haunt you for the rest of your life if you keep running away from it."

"You can't let this incident define your life. Shit happens in life, but you have to decide how you handle the situation. You have to pick yourself up and move past it. It will be hard, but it will be worth it. I mean I used to be a sad kid that would keep everything bottled in, but now I'm a very happy person."

I knew he was right. "Thank you so much, Ethan. You have done so much for me... you don't even know it."

"Really, how so?" Ethan asked.

"The whole week we were in Portland I felt like the girl I was before shit happened. This happy and hopeful girl."

"Aly, I'm glad I could help you out," Ethan said with a smile. He scratched the back of his head. "I'm sorry that I have been acting like nothing happened. I didn't know you had all of that going on in your mind and me acting weird probably didn't help you out. As much as I want to deny it, I can't. I'm still in love with you. I tried to get over you by moving on to Katie, but it didn't work. I can't stop thinking about you. About your smile and your laugh. About how much fun we had together in Portland. When I stole some of your food or when we fell on top of each other. I can't stop thinking about the kiss either. I don't ever want to stop thinking about it Aly, because I'm in love with you so deeply and can't see myself without you."

I felt a tear start to run down my face again.

"I want to kiss you again and make you feel better. I hate seeing you sad and lonely," Ethan said. I was captivated by those hazel eyes and started to smile. I was happy to have Ethan back in my life.

"I'm happy to have you back to normal, Ethan."

He laughed and messed up my hair. "You too, neighbor." We looked at each other. Ethan then softly asked, "Can I kiss you?" He put one hand on my cheek. I decided to put my past behind me and move forward, so I leaned in and kissed Ethan. He was shocked, but realized my answer. He kissed back. The kiss started to grow deeper and deeper. Ethan moved out of his chair and I fell back onto the bed. I ran my hands through Ethan's hair.

He stopped kissing me. "Aly, are you okay with this?"

I looked at him. "I want this." Ethan was shocked. I started to kiss him again. I took off his shirt. When I saw him shirtless across my room or even back in the hotel room, it was weird. This time it was different. I felt safe in his arms. Ethan ran his hand up my thigh. This was the first time I didn't have a flashback when a guy touched me. I knew I was starting to move forward. Ethan took off my shirt.

"You have a condom right?" He grabbed one out of his wallet. I looked at his chest. I ran my hand from the top of Ethan's chest to his stomach. We looked at each other. I looked at his eyes and smiled. *Thank you, Ethan Price.*

"I love you, Aly Pisano."

I wrapped my arms around his neck and kissed him deeper.

We fell onto the bed and spent the night in each other's arms.

TWELVE

Sunday: 7:30am

I woke up and realized where I was. My eyes looked over to my left and saw Ethan next to me. He had no shirt on and under the sheets I was naked. He was still sleeping, so I threw the sheets over a little. Once my clothes were on, I headed out the door quietly. *Goodbye Ethan.* I went back to my house and realized my mom wasn't home, so I headed up to my room. I threw my stuff on the ground and changed into different clothes. I lay down on my bed and looked up at the ceiling, realizing: *Ethan and I slept together.* I closed my eyes, remembering that Ethan kissed me again. This kiss was different from the last one. This one felt like it was healing me in a way. My mind started to slow down and drift back into deep slumber.

When I woke up, I looked at my phone and saw that it was ten. I got out of bed and prepared for the day. The water finally warmed up, so I got in and washed my face too. I got out and wrapped a towel around myself. My hair was wet, so a braid it was. My stomach was calling for food. As I was about to leave my room, my phone made a noise. I saw a text message from my dad. *Coming over to the house to see you and your mom later, can't wait to see you.* I was shocked. The last time my parents were together was back when I was sixteen. That meeting didn't go so well. I decided to wear leggings and a t-shirt. I headed downstairs and saw my mom cooking breakfast.

"Why is dad coming over?" I asked as I sat at the countertop.

"We need to talk about college and how much he will be paying for your education," She said as she put pancakes on a plate. She put the plate down in front of me and walked back to the sink to wash the dishes.

"Mom, you don't have to do this." She stopped washing the dishes and turned around.

"It's okay, Aly. I will be fine. It's not like last time."

"Okay." I ate my breakfast.

12:30pm

I heard a knock on the door. I opened it and saw my dad standing right in front of me. He smiled and said, "Hi Aly, can I come in?"

"Sure." He walked in and I led him to the back porch. My mom was sitting there reading a newspaper. She looked up. "Hi, Aaron."

"Hello, Jane." They looked at each other. It was interesting to see two people who loved each other to death in the past, act so distant now. He sat down. My mom asked, "Do you need anything to drink?"

"Water would be nice," My dad said.

I got up and went to get him a glass of ice water. I came back, gave it to him, and left. I hoped my mom would be alright. The last time my dad came over was to give her divorce papers. She was already a mess and that was just the spark to the flame. She went through depression. All she would do was go to work, come home, cry, and on the weekends, drink a whole bottle of wine and fall asleep. John was able to pick up on it and helped her get better. To this day, I never wanted to see my mom that sad again.

2:00pm

I was working on homework in my room until around two. My mom called for me to come downstairs.

"What's up?" I asked.

"Sit down, Aly," She said.

"Aly…when you're over at my house something seems to be bothering you. Every time you were asleep, you muttered someone's name," My dad said. "Who's Nathan?"

I froze and dropped the glass of water I had in my hand on the ground. My mom looked at me shocked. "Aly, are you okay?"

I sighed. "I have to tell you guys something. Something about this Nathan person."

I told them how whenever I went to downtown Seattle I wasn't meeting up with Hollie or Kristen. At least not after the second time. I told them how I met Nathan at a concert and we had a connection after meeting for the first time. How I kissed him in the back of the alley, so we decided to date in secret. How I lie about going to stay with Hollie or Kristen because really I was staying with him. How I fell in love with him, but the only reason I did was because he was my happiness. How I felt like he was the only person who cared about me, while they were going through a divorce.

I looked at their faces and saw how shocked there were.

I told them how I felt like Nathan loved me just as much as I loved him. How I invited him over to the house. How he put something in my drink. How he touched me in a way I didn't like. How I blacked out and woke up not knowing what happened the night before. How Nathan was also my rapist.

Tears started coming down my cheeks. These weren't tears of sadness; these were tears of happiness. I finally told them. My parents knew what happened to me. My mom was crying and my dad was shocked. They got up and hugged me.

"Aly, I'm so sorry," My dad said. "I did this. I wasn't there for you."

"I'm so sorry, Aly," My mom said. "I didn't even know you felt so affected by the divorce because I was in my own emotions. We caused you so much pain and were so clueless to see it."

"It's okay. This incident has caused me great pain, yes, but I'm okay now," I said. "I can't let it have a hold over me anymore. This was two years ago and I'm just happy I finally was able to tell you guys."

"I have seen a change in you Aly," My mom said with a smile as she wiped the tears away. "You look like the girl you were when you were 12. That happy girl filled with so many hopes and dreams." She looked at my dad. She held out her hand. "Let's put our differences in the past, Aaron and put this guy away in jail."

"Mom...even if he went to jail I would always have to live with the fact I was raped," I said. "I have forgiven him." I really had forgiven Nathan and wanted to put it in the past. I'm sure its probably hard for him to live with the fact he raped a girl. Let alone a girl who was madly in love with him. I started to remember his face when he walked into the room. He looked sad. I think he was only acting like he was tough in front of his sister, when in truth, he was affected by it as well. A soft smile appeared on my face. *I forgive you Nathan.* I looked at my parents. "I'm ready to put it in the past. I want to move forward with life."

I closed my eyes and opened them again. The knot in my stomach came back. This time, I knew what I had to do as I ran out of my house and over to Ethan's house.

Hoping for him to be there.

THIRTEEN

Sunday: 6:00pm

I walked up to the door and rang the bell. I hoped Ethan would answer the door, so I could hug him. I'm not like your typical girl who would kiss him right when I saw him. The door opened and Ethan's sister, Abby stood in front of me.

"Hey Aly, Ethan is out of town with my dad," She said. "I don't know when he will be back." I sighed. "Okay, thanks Abby." I headed back home and headed straight up to my room. I fell onto my bed and decided to go to bed. There was no point to staying awake anymore. I drifted off to sleep, hoping to see Ethan at school tomorrow, hopefully.

Monday: 10:45am

Ethan wasn't in Creative Writing. I wanted to text him, but didn't know how to start the conversation since the last time I saw him we slept together. In math class, Preston was acting weird. He looked down at the desk as I sat in my seat. I was confused why he was acting so weird. After we went over the lesson, we were given time to work on the assignment alone. I put in my headphones and focused on my work. Preston kept looking over at me from time to time. The bell rang and we left the classroom.

"Aly, I need to say something," Preston said. I looked at him confused. "What's up?"

"After Mason punched me, he helped me home. On the way back, he explained to me why you acted the way you did. I'm so sorry for doing that to you. I'm done with that lifestyle. I don't want to be that kind of guy and I know I don't need those things to be happy. Do you forgive me?"

I was taken back from what Preston was saying. I smiled at him. "It's okay. I'm not mad at you. I know you weren't in the right mindset. It's the past. I'm glad you want to change your lifestyle."

"Yeah. My friends actually are supportive of my decision. It's really thanks to you Aly. Thank you so much!" He hugged me and smiled. I hugged him back. I was glad Preston wanted to change his ways. We talked about hanging out again before going separate ways.

At lunch, I looked at Ethan's empty seat and wanted to know where he was. Mason tapped my shoulder to bring me back to the conversation. I smiled and talked with my friends.

3:00pm

I had work from three until nine. Once off, I went straight up to my room. I wanted to know where Ethan was, but part of me was scared to figure out where he was. I closed my eyes and hoped this week would go by faster.

Friday: 9:00am

I woke up and decided to look nice. It was Friday and the whole week I had been slacking. My outfit was these ripped jeans and a loose t-shirt with a red flannel. Topping it off, with my red Converse and my braided hair like always. I looked at myself in the mirror and smiled. For the first time in so long, I was really happy to look at myself and love what I saw. I grabbed my backpack and keys and left my room. In the kitchen, I grabbed a banana and a bottle of water. Then headed to my car, hoping to see Ethan's car. *No Car. No*

Ethan. I got in my car and looked at the time. *Maybe he left early.* I buckled up and drove off to school. When I got there, his car wasn't there. I sighed and realized the day was going to be long. I headed onto campus with headphones in my ear.

After I left school, I decided to head to work for a few hours to earn extra money. It was nice being back in the bookstore and helping Mr. Thomas with a few college students looking for books. When we got less busy, he told me I was done for the day. I looked at the clock and realized it was only five, but headed home anyway. I pulled into my driveway and sighed. *Ethan. I miss you.* I got out of the car and grabbed my purse. Ethan's car still wasn't there. *There is a bottle of wine in the fridge calling my name.* I started to get my house key ready, when all of a sudden, I heard someone say, "Well, hey there neighbor, why do you look so glum?" I looked up and dropped my stuff on the ground. Ethan was standing there in front of me with his gleeful smile on his face. I was speechless.

"Why are you looking at me like that, neighbor?" He raised his eyebrow. I hugged him. He laughed. "Did you miss me? I got a text from someone saying a specific person missed me a lot." *Mason I hate you, but thank you as well.* I let go of him and rolled my eyes.

"It's okay, you can admit it. I mean, I missed you too." I looked at him and hit his arm.

"Where did you go?"

"I got into Chapman University, so I had to go down for a week to fill out stuff. My mom took me. It was really nice seeing her again. Man, do I miss her." I was shocked and really happy for him. Ethan smiled.

"I'm happy to be back here."

I laughed. "Why?"

"Well, because I get to do this." He moved closer to me and kissed me. I smirked. "So?" He stopped and scratched the back of his head. "Well, you did kind of leave me alone in bed on Sunday. You didn't even tell me you were leaving, and I wanted to do that the next time I saw you." I laughed. He laughed as well. My eyes looked into his hazel eyes and remembered how safe there were whenever I was with him. So, I told him.

"I love you. I love you so much Ethan Price." He was shocked. "I love you so much that everyday I keep falling more and more in love with you. You have helped me bring back the part of me I lost when I was raped and gave up on love, so thank you Ethan. Thank you." Tears started running down my face. This tears were tears of joy because I was finally moving from my past. Ethan wiped my tears away and smiled at me.

"Thank you for coming into my life." He looked at me

"I should be thanking you for being you, Aly Pisano." He kissed me and I kissed back. The kiss lasted for a few seconds because we remembered we were outside. We laughed.

"Let's go inside," I said as we walked into my house.

8:00pm

Ethan stayed for dinner. After dinner, he hung out with me in my room since it was a Friday night. We played video games. He gave me the controller and started to tickle me. I tickled him back. He ended up on top of me and started to kiss me. When he moved to my neck, I realized where this was about to lead to.

"Wait," I said as I got up from the floor. "I want to finish my writing assignment." Ethan smiled. "Fine, be speedy fast." He lay on my bed as I sat down in front my desk. I opened my laptop and started my assignment.

What I learned this year?

If you told me at the beginning of the year, I would fall in love with my best friend, I would have told you that's crazy because love is a controllable emotion. I would have told you all the reasons why love is an incident. The incident that caused my parents to love each other, but somehow let my dad walk out on his family. That caused me to fall in love with someone I shouldn't have and ended up heartbroken. That caused my best friend so much pain when she falls for the wrong person. I would have made you feel like loving someone was a wrong thing for you to have done. My mindset changed when someone very important to me took me on a trip. This person brought back the girl who believed. Who would dance without a care in the world. Who had hope. Who hoped to fall in love like her parents did in high school. Who hoped to never feel sadness. This person brought back the girl who had happiness in her heart and you could tell. Over the past few months, I have gotten to experience life in a different light all thanks to this person. I know what happiness is again. What conquering a dark past is like. What happiness for divorced parents looks like. I even know what it feels like to be completely hopeless in love with a person. I got to say, its pretty great to be in love with your best friend. I don't know what will happen between us in the next few years or next few hours, but I want to treasure what I have with him now.

So, if you asked me what have I learned this year, I would have to tell you: you can't let one incident determine how things happen in life. If something emotional happens in your life, you have to move past it. It will take time, but once you do it's a great feeling. Also, I have learned you honestly can't control who you fall in love with, but you do control how you go about these feelings. Yes, love is a scary feeling because it's unpredictable. It's happiness. It's sadness. It's joy. It's beauty. It's ugly. It's an emotion like no other. Love might seem like an incident in disguise, but I promise you one thing. When you do meet someone who loves you just as much as you love them, it's the best feeling in the world.

I promise you that.

A.P

I closed my laptop and looked over to my bed. Ethan looked like he was asleep. I walked over to my bed and lay down next to him. I cuddled up next to him and played with his hair a bit.

"I love you," Ethan said softly.

"I love you, too."

I looked at him and realized something. I don't know if we will be able to make it work or if we even have a chance of trying it out. I mean, there was only a few months left of high school and then we leave for college. Then, I looked at Ethan and smiled. I don't know where this relationship will go, but I guess we will have to see.

Won't we?

The End

Acknowledgement

I want to thank my facilitators, Ryan Pine, Shari Arnold, and Lindsey Sheppard for helping me make this book possible.

I want to thank my 12th grade English teacher, Jessica Sprecher for helping me out and giving me the chance to write a book as my senior project

I want to thank Bri Ferrelli. You are one of my best friends and without your help, I won't have been able to come up with an amazing turn of events so thank you so much Bri.

I want to thank my amazing, supportive friends: Penny Davenport, Daniela Martinez, Sarah McDaniel, Anna Morris, Wendy Guajardo, Katie Whitlow, Carine Seudieu, Elvira Prozorac, and the list goes on. Thank you so much for being there for me and keeping me motivated through out the whole thing.

I want to thank my family. I wouldn't have been able to write this book without my older brother, Nsikan Akpan and Itoro Akpan helping me along the way.

I want to thank my mom, Nko Akpan. You helped me so much from meeting with my facilitators to pushing me to finish writing and I can't thank you enough. Even if it doesn't seem like it, I love you very dearly and thank you so much mom.

Lastly, I want to thank my role model, John Green. You have inspired me to write and I look up to you very much. Thank you for writing amazing books and helping me realize what makes me who I am today.

H.A

ABOUT HANNA AKPAN

Hanna Akpan is the author of The Incident. She is from Atlanta, Georgia, but will be attending college in the fall of 2016 out of state. She wrote The Incident back in her last year of high school as her senior project. She hopes to end up in New York City, writing for magazines, and most of all, continue writing books.

Made in the USA
Charleston, SC
01 May 2016